© Copyright Donald Townsend 2020
Published by Glorybound Publishing
SAN 256-4564
10 9 8 7 6 5 4 3 2 1
Printed in the United States of America
ISBN 9798672088624
Library of Congress Cataloging-in-Publication data is available
on file.
Townsend, Donald, 1963-
      Frozen N Time/Donald Townsend
      Includes biographical reference.
1. Thriller Novel
I. Title

www.gloryboundpublishing.com

Cover Design: Dave Matthews

CONTACT REFU

Refu63@protomail.com

Written by: Donald Townsend
Edited by: Donald Townsend
Cover Design: Dave Matthews

Frozen N Time

by Donald Townsend

A Refu story

Glorybound Publishing
Camp Verde, Arizona
Released 2020

WHY DO I WRITE

I write to enlight make your brain ignite
Making your mind take flight
 On a cosmic level of poetic flow
Unfolding knowledge of past present and future
Ripping a moment in time to scratch a groove in your mind
Twisting and changing the way you think things should be or
appear to be
Poetry can cause your mind to blink
And start you to think about words that are genetically
linked
To penetrate the cranium deposit thoughts into the brain
that's attached to the pituitary gland
To make you become a fan of that which you hear which is
poetry
I write to release the truth that dances on my tongue like a
bad taste
If I don't spit it out, it makes me a concealer of the truth
Of how I've seen poetry elevates a new level of
consciousness
Giving you visual imagery of the words that will split your
dome right down the middle
I've seen poets make the mic glow and vibrate from a raw
tongue lashing of truth
Unleashing a time-release capsule of poetic medicine
To feed the masses to awaken them from sleep with the high
pitch sound of energized vibration
That's pulsating the ingredients of consciousness
I'm telling the history of highlights and insights of my life
That paints a masterpiece picture with poetic words
That transforms the art of listening
By tapping into senses, you didn't even know you had
What's really unique, I write in my sleep
After my physical catches up with my spirit, I do it twice
You call it déjà vu, I call it a spiritual lesson unfolding within

me
I write to recite real thought
Mind expansion is what I seek Because words are spells of age-old allusion that keeps you trapped
It could take a lifetime for one to be released for the thing that clouds your judgment
Listening is an art that some will never master, only because they choose not to
I write because sometimes my thoughts are like blank pieces of white paper with no meaning
But once the black ink explodes on the page, only then do my words become a reality
Enhancing a shift in my matrix That's why I write to feed the mic with confidence and self-pride
In broad daylight in the middle of the night even with a flashlight
Putting words together is like directing an orchestra
Only I know the highs and lows of the masterpiece that flows from my soul only to warm the spirit and ignite the mind like a star system
That tweaks the consciousness beyond sight to transcend belief structures of falsehood
Living in the know of factual evidence that can't be disputed
To know and know you know is a smile of priceless confidence that can't be disputed
I seek knowledge like hell seek souls
Only you are responsible for your mind, body, and soul It may seem like someone else has control
That's only because you've allowed them to everybody plays the blame game when it comes to the spiritual essence of life
Everybody wants to pass on what's has been passed on to them with the acceptance of the truth
Instead of due diligence of research and study
This is one of the reasons why I read write research and converse

Because I want to know how deep does the rabbit hole
really goes
That's why I write
Life is poetry

Dedicated to

Calvin Hilson & Jerry Eppenger gone too soon

Acknowledgments

First things, first. I am in the all and the all is in me. I'm part of the all, and all is a part of me. I can succeed as a part of the all, or I can fail as an individual. All exist within the all, you can add to it, and you cannot take away from it. Because all exist within it. All praises are due to the all The Most High. I want to thank Laura Rongomas for her encouraging words. My immediate family. My brother, Michael Townsend, was extremely helpful in my mission of getting this book done. My closest friends, with encouraging words. The journey continues. As my imagination flows. I want to thank every individual that has spent their hard-earned money on the purchase of my book, Enjoy.

Introduction

In early 1900s Chicago, the roaring thunder and crackling lightning accompanied by heavy rain was so intense that it seemed as if the earth itself would split open. Despite the brewing storm outside, the Hemmingbird factory created a cozy and inviting ambiance. However, even the wash of rain couldn't cleanse the malevolence and darkness that resided deep within Fred Hemmingbird's soul. Fred, with skilled hands, diligently repaired a box camera and meticulously cleaned its viewfinder. He sprayed the camera body with precision and used an air compressor to ensure its pristine condition. Frustration mounted as a flickering light above his workstation tormented him intermittently. He glanced up at the erratic light, annoyance etching his face. Cleaning the shutter mechanism, adjusting the aperture, and carefully placing small screws around the lens, Fred applied a tad too much force. The screwdriver slipped from his grasp, impaling his left index finger. "Shit!" Fred exclaimed, as blood dripped onto the camera lens and its components. He peered down over his glasses, sucking on his injured finger and muttered another expletive, "Son of a bitch." Coincidentally, Fred's boss strolled by at that moment and inquired about his wellbeing. "Fred, is everything okay?" the boss asked with concern. Fred quickly composed himself and replied,

"Yes, everything is fine!" Fred worked in a camera factory, known for his meticulousness and cleanliness. However, behind his facade, Fred grappled with a complex personality that others described as fraught with negative thoughts and emotions. Some even labeled him as having multiple characters, akin to what we now understand as bipolar disorder. His attention to detail bordered on obsessional at times, displaying traits of OCD. Although the part of Chicago where Fred resided during the early 1900s appeared serene on the surface, it concealed a dark underbelly that left people afraid to venture out alone. The police had failed to solve fifteen gruesome murders, creating an atmosphere of pervasive fear. When Fred met his fate in February 1909, the people branded him a mad killer, responsible for mutilating victims beyond recognition. The authorities never apprehended him, but mounting evidence and newspaper articles began to point accusatory fingers at Fred Hemmingbird.

Table of contents

The camera buy page ……………………..11

The surprise at the park page …………..25

The rundown page ……………………43

The investigation page ………………..61

Everyone's connected page …………… 89

A visit from the past page …………… 111

Mind game page ……………………137

I never knew ……………………… 149

The Camera Buy

The year was 2020 when a particular camera manufacturer introduced a new camera featuring vintage glass lenses. Unfortunately, the camera did not perform well in the market, leading to its discontinuation. Limited to only around 100 units, this camera was called the OGPS560. It was during a weekend camera shopping excursion with my friend Mark that I stumbled upon one of these rare cameras at a pawnshop.

Mark, a notorious jokester, always had a smile on his face and referred to everyone as "chief." I don't believe he ever took anything seriously in his life. Standing at 5'10" and weighing around 145 pounds, Mark had short wavy hair, brown skin, long eyelashes, and blinked an average of 70 times per minute. He sported small square-framed glasses and often complained about dry eyes. Whenever Mark got excited, his favorite saying was, "You can bet that!" He would repeat it tirelessly, grabbing your hand, pulling you close, and emphasizing that line. Mark's favorite shoe brand was black Chuck Taylor All-Stars, and on that day, he wore blue jeans and an orange T-shirt that read "Power to All People." On that beautiful day, with the temperature at a pleasant 75 degrees, the sun hid behind the clouds. Our intention was to find a camera to capture and immortalize the memories of our senior year. Thus, we found ourselves at Sal's Pawn Shop, a massive 4000 square foot establishment. The floor's shine was blinding as we walked through the entrance, accompanied by the background melody of jazz music. To the left, there was a section displaying jewelry in glass mirror cases, with walls adorned with every imaginable accessory. On the right side, a variety of televisions and computers were on display. In the back stood the service counter, where customers settled their payments. I marveled at the vast assortment of items one could find in a pawnshop. To the right of the service counter, a case held various cameras and games. Mark made his way towards the glass display

"Hey, Marcus, maybe this Polaroid will suit you, man!" Mark said, laughing with a mischievous smirk on his face.

"No can do, man. But maybe you should get it and take some pictures of that peculiar dog of yours. Isn't it some strange hybrid of a rat and a rabbit? And who names their dog Bootsy!" I retorted.

Mark was influenced by old-school music and had an admiration for Bootsy Collins. I couldn't resist the opportunity to jokingly associate his dog with Bootsy Collins.

"No way, come on, man, don't talk about my dog like that."

"I'm just saying, you named that dog Bootsy. Scratching my head, I couldn't help but think to myself, "Man, I really like that." I was a young man with a dark brown complexion, short wavy hair, and stood at a height of 5'10" weighing 165 pounds. My broad nose, brown eyes, small mole over my left eyebrow, full lips, and bright white teeth that were proudly displayed since getting my braces off last summer. People often described me as an all-around athlete. I excelled in football, basketball, and track, while also maintaining straight A grades. Science was my passion, and I proudly achieved a place on the Dean's list during my sophomore and junior years. Many considered me the smartest student in the entire school. No matter the subject, I was always enthusiastic about learning and exploring.

In the moment, I found myself standing in front of a display case in a pawnshop, which held an empty black backpack, the perfect place for my new camera. Dressed in a colorful short sleeve button-up shirt, blue jeans, and dark blue running shoes, I felt an appreciation for everything I had ever received. My mind was set on capturing photos of all the people I would miss once high school came to an end. The pawnshop was filled with various cameras, but one particular camera stood out amongst the rest. With a big smile, I exclaimed to myself, "This is it!" I gently ran my left hand over my wavy hair, displaying my 32 gleaming teeth as I continued to smile. Fixated on the camera, I approached the guy behind the counter, whose name tag read Sal.

"Excuse me, Sal, sir. Can I take a look at this camera?" I politely inquired.

"Sure thing, kid. You seem to really like that camera," Sal replied.

"Yes, sir. I'm drawn to this camera," I gestured towards it. "May I see it, please?" The pawnshop was asking for $150 for the camera, but deep down, I knew I wouldn't pay that price. The tag on the camera revealed that it had been sitting in the shop for almost a year.

"Can you let it go for $75?" I proposed, hoping for a positive response, although I anticipated Sal would reject such a low offer.

"No can do, no way no how. I paid $100 for it, and I won't let it go for less than that," Sal affirmed, his lips tightly sealed.

Sal resembled a mobster with his black slacks, short-sleeved light blue shirt, large, black-framed glasses, and comb-over hairstyle. His noticeable dandruff and thick eyebrows added to his distinguishable appearance. Despite his perpetual sleepy expression, customers flocked to his pawnshop for the best deals.

I tried one last attempt. "What about a hundred dollars, no tax, straight out the door?" I proposed, hoping to strike a deal.

"Come on, kid, you're busting my balls here. $110. I have to make a profit from my products," Sal joked, revealing a bit of his business-savvy demeanor. Listening to his negotiation tactic, I couldn't help but think, "He really sounds like the mob."

With a wrinkled forehead, I attempted to appear helpless, pleading, "All I have is a hundred dollars. Come on, Sal."

"Okay, kid. Tell me, why do you want this camera so badly?" Sal inquired, taking a step back and crossing both of his arms. and his right hand holding his chin, Sal looked at Marcus as I explained my reason for wanting the camera. "I'm going to be taking photos of the people I'm going to miss after I graduate. You know, in my senior year of high school, before I head off to college," I said, hunching my shoulders in an attempt to persuade Sal to lower the price.

"Okay, kid, that's a good enough reason. This time, I'll let you have it for a hundred dollars. But next time, whatever you buy, I want an extra $10," Sal agreed, giving in to my request.

"Okay, cool. Does it come with a charger?" I asked, hoping that Martha, Sal's assistant, would be able to find one.

"Let me check. Hey, Martha, do we have a charger for this camera?" Sal called out to her, and Martha walked up, took the camera from him, and headed to the back to find the charger.

"I'll check and see," Martha confirmed.

"Okay, kid, here you go. Martha found the charger. Now go and take some good pictures. That's a good camera, kid. By the way, nice shirt you're wearing," Sal complimented me as he handed me the camera.

"Thank you, I appreciate everything. Thanks a lot, Mr. Sal," I replied gratefully. Turning to Mark, I exclaimed, "Man, I can't wait to get home and charge up my camera!"

"Yeah, that's a nice camera, boy!" Mark exclaimed, his smile stretching across his face. I was bubbling with excitement about my new camera and couldn't wait to show it to my mom and dad. My mom was a pharmacist, and my dad owned a small auto mechanic shop. They had been happily married for 22 years, and I was their only child. We lived in a middle-class suburban home with three bedrooms and 2 ½ baths on a 1 ½ acre lot. The quiet suburban area was populated by neighbors who mostly kept to themselves. In front of the house, there was a 3-foot-high block wall fence with metal detailing between the brick pillars. Tall bushes grew behind the wall, and there was a plum tree on the front left side of the house, along with a large shade tree on the other side.

My mom, Sandra, was a stunning woman, standing at 5'6" and weighing 130 pounds. She had light skin, curly dark black hair, a petite nose, and full lips. Her upbeat personality radiated as she jogged around the neighborhood each morning, turning heads in her workout gear. On the other hand, was my dad named Paul, still dressed in blue jeans and a white T-shirt. My dad, known as Pops, always seemed to have a thousand white T-shirts, and he constantly kept busy either around the house or in his shop. Pops was highly respected in the neighborhood, standing at 6'4" and weighing 220 pounds. He had a calm demeanor and was cool as a fan, rarely getting upset about anything. In his younger days, he had played college basketball, and to this day, I couldn't beat him in a game. Everything he did seemed to happen in slow motion. With his dark skin, pearly white teeth, and goatee, he exuded a sharpness that earned him the nickname "Slow Motion." Mark and I walked into the house, eager to share my newfound treasure To the right was the family room where we all gathered to watch videos on a projector screen hanging from the ceiling. There was a shelf against the left wall, stocked with movies and videos. The room boasted four comfortable leather recliner lounge chairs, positioned about 10 feet away from the screen. My father was a fan of action movies, evident by the various movie posters adorning the walls of the movie room. On the left side of the screen, there was a 24x36 print photo of the Gladiator, while on the right side, a poster of The Godfather proudly hung. Pops considered those to be his favorite films and had a few other posters scattered throughout the room. At that moment, he was relaxing and enjoying a ballgame, while my mother comfortably reclined in a brown lounge chair, with her feet resting on the armrest, draped across Paul's lap. Paul, immersed in the game, seemed quite animated, crunching his toes into the deep beige shag carpet and passionately voicing his opinions.

"Move the ball! That's a bad shot! Push the ball, man!" he yelled enthusiastically. I always told him he should consider becoming a coach.

"Mom, Pops, you won't believe the camera I found with the hundred dollars you gave me. Check it out!" I exclaimed, turning their attention towards me.

My mother turned, taking off her glasses and looking over the chair. "Oh, baby, that's nice! Now you can take some great shots of your friends!" she exclaimed with a smile.

"Yeah, I know it's going to be amazing!" I responded, grinning from ear to ear as I stared at my new camera.

"Let me check it out, son," my father said, inspecting the camera from different angles.

"Nice, nice," he complimented, handing it back to me. "You did well for yourself, son."

My dad suddenly started striking poses, exclaiming, "Catch this! Catch that! I should be a model because I look good!" A big smile spread across his face, while Mark stood nearby with his right hand on his face.

"What's wrong, Mark? Ask Paul," my dad said, looking at Mark with amazement, shaking his head.

"Yeah, Mr. Davis," Mark blinked rapidly, "you look like you should be modeling underwear for Sears."

"See, son, that's your friend," my dad said, nodding and looking at Mark with amusement.

"My pops is right; something is wrong with you, man," I chimed in.

"Hey, I don't know! I'm just saying," Mark defended himself.

Marcus looked at his dad and said, "Okay, true pops, you look good, but not as good as me. As soon as I get the camera charged, I'm going to take some pictures of you and mom," Mark declared, heading to the kitchen to get a glass of water. Paul glanced at his son, shaking his head rapidly from side to side and closing his eyes. He then looked down at his wife.

"Baby, you know, I think there's something off about that kid Mark. I hope he's not hiding anything or, you know, playing for the other team.

But anyway, alright, son, that sounds good. I'm ready too; I was made for the flash, you know," Paul responded, a hint of humor in his voice.

"I'm going upstairs to plug in my camera. Seriously, something's wrong with you, posing like a Sears underwear model," Marcus said to Mark, rolling his eyes.

"Come on, let's go upstairs!" Walking past the family room, the house opened up with a high vaulted ceiling and a pleasant scent of fresh lemongrass in the air. To the left, there were eight stairs that led to the middle landing, where the second step would always squeak. Ten more stairs turned right, leading straight up to the upper level of the house. From there, the entire hallway was visible, spanning from left to right. The three bedrooms on the top floor were in view: the master bedroom to the left, the guest bedrooms to the right, and my bedroom straight ahead. The staircase was adorned with white and dark brown oak railings on both sides. Stepping into my room, it was impeccably clean. I had a queen-size bed against the left wall, a computer desk against the right wall, and a poster of my favorite football team, the Bears, hung above my bed. Right by the door, I kept a black folding chair where I draped my jacket.

"Do you think your dad is going to think I'm gay just because I mentioned him modeling Sears underwear?" Mark scratched his head, blinking rapidly.

"Dude, something's definitely wrong with you," I replied as Mark raised his eyebrows in surprise. He then took a step closer until he was about half a foot away from me.

"No, no, no, something's wrong with you. One thing's for sure, all those girls at school are going to want us to take pictures of them. You can bet on that!" Mark exclaimed, blinking furiously and flashing a wide grin.

"Man, watch out! Get out of my face!" I said, and we both burst into laughter. Two hours later, the camera's battery was fully charged, and I couldn't stop clicking away, capturing images of everything.

"Mark, look at how amazing these pictures look! They're so clear," I exclaimed, with Mark standing beside me, smiling and blinking rapidly.

"Oh, we're in for some fun. I can't wait to snap shots of that gorgeous ass Tonya Jenkins! Man, she's so fine!" Mark exclaimed, causing me to shake my head in amusement "Right, right, you're right. Tonya is incredibly attractive," I whispered, putting my hand over my mouth. "And she's always at the park, playing volleyball." I had a blank expression on my face as I daydreamed. Mark noticed and glanced at me, blinking rapidly before pausing and looking at me over his glasses. "Hey man, what's wrong with you? Snap out of it before you embarrass yourself and start drooling," he said, bursting into laughter and holding his stomach.

Laughing along, I wiped my mouth and replied, "Come on, Mark, I'm not drooling." I checked my hand to see if there was anything on it.

Still laughing hysterically, Mark exclaimed, "Dude, I saw you wipe your mouth."

"Come on, stop joking around, Mark. Let's head over to Griffin Park, you crazy fool. I want to see my camera in action," I said, playfully wiping my hands on his shirt. "You're such a fool," Mark chuckled.

As the sun emerged from behind the clouds, the weather couldn't have been better; it was 82 degrees. Griffin Park, the city's oldest and largest park, was a massive 38,000-acre space. The park was a maze, with numerous big trees and a beautiful flower garden surrounded by a three-foot brick fence. Concrete benches were scattered all around, and you'd always find someone taking photos in the garden. The park even had its streets with names. It offered various amenities, including eight basketball courts, baseball diamonds, a nine-hole Frisbee golf course, a skateboard park, football and soccer fields, sand volleyball nets, a dog run, and a track encircling the entire park. Picnic spots and family barbecue grills were always occupied, and high school kids often gathered by the lake to feed ducks or relax on the dedicated park benches, each engraved with a special dedication. There were poetry sessions and occasional live band performances, making Griffin Park the go-to place for the entire town.

The park was bustling with people, walking, talking, cycling, and during the summers, my friends and I would spend the entire day there. Although it was only a 5-minute bus ride from our house, Mark and I mostly preferred to walk, discussing our plans on the way. When we arrived, we would pass the basketball courts before reaching the lake area. On this particular day, a five-on-five pickup basketball game was underway, and Franklin Pete, an all-American basketball player from our school, called out to me.

" Yo, Marcus, that's a nice camera on your shoulder. Mind taking a shot?" he asked, holding the ball above his head with one hand. "Sure thing!" I said, pulling the camera strap across my shoulder and capturing some shots. "Got you, man," I spoke as I clicked the shutter. "No doubt, Marcus!" Franklin exclaimed, throwing a fist pump.

"See, Marcus, everyone wants a picture and wants to talk to you when you have a camera in your hand," Mark remarked, looking at my camera. "You're right. Look, there she is, man. Miss beautiful Tonya Jenkins," Mark said, touching his baseball cap and blinking rapidly. "She's so gorgeous that you involuntarily say her name twice: Tonya Jenkins, Tonya

Jenkins."

"Wow, man, she's coming over here," I replied, grinning from ear to ear. "Look, here she comes!" I described Tonya, her captivating features and stunning figure, expressing my admiration.

"Hi, Marcus, hi, Mark," Tonya greeted us at the same time. "Hello, Tonya," we both responded.

"Marcus, I see you have a new toy," Tonya said flirtatiously, referring to my camera.

"Yeah, just something I want to use to capture photos of all the people I'll miss when I go off to college," I thought to myself with a smile.

"Oh, Marcus, that's a great idea. I've always wanted to take some artistic nude photos," Tonya playfully remarked with a big smile on her face.

Surprised by her comment, I exclaimed, "Come on, girl, you better stop."

"I just finished running a couple of laps. Spent 69 dollars on my sweatsuit, and the look on your faces was priceless. Just kidding, but the look on your faces is priceless. I wish I had a photo of that. Cause these are the things that MasterCard brings," Tonya said, trailing off and chuckling. Amused by her words, I chuckled to myself, thinking, "Girl, you really know how to surprise me."

"You know, I was going to devour you like a snicker bar," I remarked with a stutter, pretending to be overwhelmed.

"Don't play with me, Tonya" said, Mark blinking rapidly and holding his chest playfully, as if he was about to pass out.

"Damn, Tonya, you're making me heat up too fast. You're dangerous, no doubt about it," I said, standing there, grinning from ear to ear, silently telling myself that she would eventually tire of playing games with me.

"You know what, I'd love a couple of photos of you if you don't mind, Tonya," I finally gathered the courage to ask.

"You know I don't mind, but let me take a few pictures with Mark first," Tonya responded, adding excitement to the situation.

"Oh, Tonya, now I won't be able to say anything to him," Mark playfully protested, blinking rapidly and holding his chest.

"Come on, Marcus, no need to be jealous. I told you, I'm the man," replied Mark, constantly moving and blinking, stirring the playful acting joyful.

While Mark was captivated, I couldn't help but laugh and join in, saying, "You need to stay still so I can take your picture."

Mark, lost in his admiration for Tonya, just looked at her up and down, appearing to be in a trance. In his mind, he thought, "She wants me, I just know it," walking with a confident stride and shaking his head from side to side. "You can bet that," he added.

"So, let me take a few solo shots of you, Tonya," I suggested.

"Okay, how do you want me to pose?" she asked, smiling at me. Tonya crossed her legs, put her hands together over her head, and leaned to the left. "How's this, Marcus?" she asked in a seductive voice. Her butt to hip ratio was unreal.

"That's great, just be yourself," I replied, and I proceeded to capture twenty-five stunning photos of her.

"Thanks so much, Marcus! Will you give me copies of those photos?" Tonya asked, grateful for the photoshoot.

"Of course," I assured her.

"Alright, guys, I've got to run. I'll see you soon," Tonya said as she bid us goodbye.

"Okay, Tonya," we both responded.

"Tonya, can I talk to you for a moment?" I asked, walking close to her so Mark could not hear our conversation.

"Sure, Marcus, what's up?" she replied, turning towards me. I gathered the courage to express my feelings, saying, "You know, I've been attracted to you for a long time. What do you think, can we get together?"

"Yes, we definitely can! I've been waiting for you to ask. I've dropped so many hints, Marcus," Tonya responded, gently rubbing my neck and head with both hands, with a flirty air. "Call me tonight," she added, giving me a kiss on the cheek.

"Marcus, what was that all about? Today was a good day, my brother," Marcus said, joining in with high-fives and handshakes.

"Yes, it sure was, my brother. It's getting late; we should head home," I suggested.

"Absolutely," Mark agreed.

"Right, right," I replied. "Marks, house was on the street before my house. we always seem to get home faster coming back than going there."

"Alright, man. We'll check out the pictures tomorrow," Mark

said, giving me a thumb-up.

"Sounds good. Peace," I said, and we exchanged handshakes. "See you tomorrow, my brother." Mark turned onto his street, and four minutes later, I walked through the front door of my house. To the left of the movie room was the living room, always immaculate and unused. I walked into the movie room, placed my camera on the table next to my dad's favorite chair, and headed upstairs for a good night's sleep.

Surprise at the Park

Early the next morning, it was a Sunday, and my parents were getting ready for church. They never forced me to go, but they would often suggest that I attend occasionally. As I walked down the stairs in my t-shirt, socks, and underwear, the enticing smell of breakfast filled the air, prompting my mom to ask about the pictures I took at the park the previous day.

Leaning her head to the side, with raised eyebrows showing interest, she inquired, "So, how did the pictures at the park go yesterday?"

I replied with a smile, saying, "It went great. I took some nice shots of Tonya Jenkins."

She then questioned me if I was going to church, to which I replied, "No, I don't think so. Let me grab my camera to show you the photos and capture some shots of you and dad in your church attire."

As I made my way across the shaggy carpet, I reached out to grab my camera but accidentally received an electric shock both from the camera and the lens. Though I thought nothing of it at the moment, I didn't realize that a yellow haze had covered the camera screen. Dismissing the idea of showing her the photos, my mom said, "Never mind, baby. I'll look at them later. Your father and I are getting ready for church. We'll see you as soon as we get back."

"Okay, mom, I'll see you and the well-dressed folks later," I replied with a slight grin. At that moment, it struck me that I had forgotten to charge my camera the previous night. Around 10:30, my friend Mark arrived at the door. I greeted him and informed him that my parents had already left. He eagerly asked, "What did they cook for breakfast?" with his eyes scanning the surroundings of the house.

"Food, man. Look at you, always on the lookout. One of these days, you're going to surprise me and not blink all the time," I jokingly replied. He blinked rapidly, asserting, "It won't be today. You can bet that. Any food left?"

"Go check in the kitchen, but don't eat it all. Save me some. I'll go upstairs and get dressed," I said. After getting dressed, I excitedly expressed to Mark, "Man, I think I want to do some of that National Geographic stuff today. I want to take some pictures of ducks at the park by the lake."

"Ducks? Seriously? Man, you've lost it. That's insanity," Mark replied, looking up in disbelief.

"Alright, duck man, let's go," Mark said, with both arms wide open in excitement.

"What's wrong with that? Animals fascinate me," I added, trying to explain my interest.

Mark responded with a mean look on his face, "Nothing, that's cool. But we're also going to take pictures of some girls, right?"

"Of course, man, I'm not that fascinated," I replied, joining in on his joking tone.

When we arrived at the park, it was a beautiful day with animals busily roaming the lake. Little did I know that this would be a day I would never forget. The park had a magnificent lake encompassing 9 acres, with a scenic walking trail surrounding it. Park benches were conveniently placed every quarter of the way along the lake. On the opposite side, tall trees and viburnum shrubs provided a picturesque backdrop. I always enjoyed the sweet aroma of blooming viburnums.

As I stood there, capturing shots of ducks swimming on the tranquil water, I suddenly heard a scream. Startled, I asked Mark if he heard it too. Looking in the direction from where the scream seemed to have come, I couldn't see anything. But then, I heard the scream again, this time begging for help. I quickly peered through the viewfinder of my camera and was horrified by what I saw—a man with a thick white rope around a woman's neck, dragging her behind the viburnum bushes.

Shocked and enraged, I started recording the scene, exclaiming, "What the fuck is going on? Look at this! He's killing her, Mark!"

Mark grabbed the camera from me and looked through the viewfinder, but he couldn't see anything. Frustrated, he accused me of playing a prank, saying, "You're going to get enough of fooling around. I don't see anything, boy. You're tripping for real."

Determined to prove him wrong, I zoomed in on the disturbing scene. "Oh my God, her legs are shaking! Now the guy is stabbing her with a knife," I gasped in horror.

Mark's expression changed to one of shock and disbelief as well. But overwhelmed by the gruesome sight, I dropped the camera and began vomiting.

Concerned, Mark exclaimed, "Oh shit, are you okay, Marcus?"

Struggling to compose myself, I responded, "What the fuck is going on? I don't see anything happening. What are you talking about, Marcus? What did you see?"

Marcus grabbed his camera, his eyes filled with fear, and without looking back, he started running towards home, terrified. I followed closely, shouting, "Wait for me!"

By the time we reached his house, tears were streaming down Mark's face. His parents had just returned home and were startled by Mark's sudden entrance.

"What the hell is wrong with you, boy? What's going on?" his father demanded, surprised.

Trying to catch my breath, I explained, "I just witnessed a murder. A man strangled a lady and stabbed her multiple times in the park—Griffin Park—and I ran away, dad."

Marcus's father, with a firm voice and a hand behind his head, urged him to calm down, "Marcus, look at me! Calm down, son. I'm here. Talk to me. What's going on?" He looked Marcus straight in the eye.

Marcus's mom, Miss Davis, appeared at the top of the stairs, concerned about the commotion. Mark burst into the house a couple of minutes later, his tears continuing to flow. Quietly, Mr. Davis addressed Mark and asked, "What's happening, son?"

Mark, still visibly shaken, replied, "I looked through the camera's viewfinder at the spot Marcus said he saw the attacker, but I didn't see anything. I looked around for a while, but then Marcus ran off, so I tried to catch up with him. That's all, but I didn't see anything."

Sitting in his father's favorite chair, Marcus hung his head, deeply saddened by the terrifying event. He seemed oblivious to everyone speaking around him; it was as if their lips were moving, but he couldn't hear a word. Meanwhile, the police—Officer Peterson and Officer Smith—arrived at the scene. Officer Peterson, a tall and broad man with a deep voice and a dark complexion, took charge of the situation.

Officer Peterson introduced himself, saying, "So, who witnessed what happened? I'm Officer Peterson."

Paul, Marcus's father, guided Officer Peterson to Marcus, introducing them. "This is Marcus. How's it going, Marcus? By the way, that's a good name. My son's name is Marcus too. I'm Officer Peterson. Before we get started, let me ask you, do you need me to call the paramedics for you? Are you okay?"

Marcus nodded, indicating that he was okay and didn't need medical attention. Officer Peterson then encouraged Marcus to take his time and share everything he saw, urging him to remember as many details as possible. Marcus began recounting the story to Officer Peterson, starting from the beginning. Officer Peterson listened attentively, taking notes. He asked Marcus about the appearance of the attacker and the victim, prompting him to recall specific details. By the end of Marcus's account, Officer Peterson requested to examine the camera. Mrs. Davis handed it over, and Officer Peterson examined the shots Marcus had taken the previous day. However, upon inspecting the camera, he couldn't find any trace of the recorded video. Scratching his head, Officer Peterson said, "There's nothing here. No video, nothing. Did someone accidentally erase it?"

Disappointed, Marcus's father asked Mark if he had witnessed anything at the park. Mark replied, "No Sir. When I looked through the camera's viewfinder where Marcus said he saw the attacker, I saw nothing. I looked around, but he ran off before I could catch up. I didn't see anything the whole time."

As the situation unfolded, I remained silently in my father's chair, consumed by sadness and shock, unable to hear or respond to anyone. All the while, the police officers were present at the scene, ready to investigate further upon Marcus's request a call from dispatch saying patrol six is on-site at the park, they have found no evidence anywhere around the lake area.

"Nothing found at the park."

"I'm telling you what I see, officer; I can't make that up."

"Marcus, do you think you might want to take a ride, down to the park with me in my partner, so you can walk us through what you see if that's all right with you, Mr. and Mrs. Davis. I also would like you to come along with us."

"Okay. Officer"

"Are you okay with that, Marcus? Are you sure you're in the condition to go back to the park?"

"I am." looking over at my mom and dad. They took that ride to the park. Marcus's parents followed alone behind the police car. With Mark in the back seat, when they arrived at the park. Officer Peterson took the scenic route, driving up on the grass to the location where Marcus directed him, from the backseat of the police car. Officer Peterson opened up the back door of the vehicle to let Marcus out. The look and fear that he saw on Marcus' face were evident. Something had happened; he didn't know what.

"Are you okay Marcus, you sure about this." Officer Peterson is towering down over Marcus.

"Yes, sir."

There were two other units in the location around the area where the crime had supposedly taken place. Marcus walked Officer Peterson back to the exact spot where he was standing when everything was happening. He then pointed towards the area, where he saw the man strangling and stabbing the woman. By this time another officer walked over to Officer Peterson telling him that they had been all around the Lake area and had not found any evidence concerning a crime.

"I was right here; right here, I saw it."

"I believe you, Marcus, okay, mom, dad, you can take them home. We're going to

look around the park, a little along to see if we can find anything; maybe we missed something, and if so, will let you know."

"You did good son," with his hand on top of Marcus' head. Okay, officer, thank you. When we made it back to the house, Marcus went into the movie room and grabbed his camera, turning it on. He then went to the menu mode, looking right at the video that he had recorded.

"Mom, dad, it's right here."

"Baby, I just don't see anything," With her hands on his shoulder.

"Neither do I, son." Looking at a blank screen. I think you should get some rest, maybe take a nap. I'm going to pull your sheets back.,

"You know that's a good idea; maybe you should lay down for a while, son. Mark, Marcus is going to lay down for a little while. Maybe you could come by later on today."

Mr. Davis walked Mark to the door.

"Get home, safe son will see you soon."

I went upstairs to lay down, I flopped down and laid back on my bed. Staring at the ceiling, eyes wide open. Ten minutes had passed; I then fell into a deep sleep. In my dream, I could hear a woman screaming. The brightness of the lime green and dark blue jogging suit was so vivid and bright. Her hands reaching out toward me, I seem to be the giant size. She was standing at the edge of the old factory. She was so small as the size of an ant. Looking up to me, she was hanging on to a clock. It read noon the clock was attached to an old factory building; the Windows were broken out. It had a look like it had been built back in the 1900s. Help me, Marcus, help me, please. Blood was running down her arms and face. She had stab wounds in her neck and back. I jumped up out of my dream, sweating. I slept through the whole day and night. I woke up two birds chirping, and to the smell of a good breakfast. I just wanted to forget about what had happened at the park. I was thinking to myself. No one could see the recording on the camera but me. I had thought about erasing it. I thought maybe it could be a malfunction in the camera. So, I decided to keep the footage; I wouldn't look at it anymore. I changed the SD card. I was so confused about how no one could see it but me. When I walked downstairs, the first thing I heard was, mom.

"There, my sleepy head, so how did you sleep last night."

"I slept well. I had a crazy dream; I can't remember it."

"Yeah, that happens to me all the time."

"Do you think dreams mean anything. Where's dad at."

"He went in early today; you need to ask him about dreams. He had a dream book, and it's somewhere around here, I don't know what he did with it."

32

"Thanks for cooking breakfast, mom, I appreciate it."

"That is nothing like cheese grits, eggs, biscuits, and turkey bacon, with orange juice, to start the day off."

I was sitting at the table drinking juice, with my pajamas on.

"You write about that. "At this time, the doorbell rang,

"Who is it?" I yelled out. It was Mark.

"Who you think. It is not UPS; you can bet that." Sticking his head in the door looking around. He walked into the house straight to the kitchen, where Mrs. Davis was standing.

"Good morning, Mrs. Davis, how are you this bright, lovely morning." With a big smile on his face blinking very fast.

"Something sure smells good up in here; you can bet that." Rubbing his hands together, licking his hips.

"Mark, would you like some breakfast." Mark points to himself.

"Who me."

"No, you. Boy don't play with me. this morning."

"Yes, I would Mrs. Davis, I thought you'd never ask Oooooo Wee! Marcus, you got a good mom. My mom doesn't cook like this in the morning."

Mrs. Davis puts Mark's plate on the table. Mark looked at Mrs. Davis and blinked about 20 times in one second. "Thank you, Jesus, and thank you to Mrs. Davis."

"Child, something is wrong with you, all that blinking. I'm going upstairs." Ms. Davis walked out of the kitchen, headed

33

upstairs. While eating his food, he is continually blinking.

"Man, you know, you scared me yesterday." Pointing his finger at Marcus, eating on toast.

"Yeah, I'm okay. I think I'm going to stay in the house for a couple of days. After I get out of school."

"Okay, that's cool, you know Wednesday, the girls got a volleyball game." Rubbing his peach fuzz around his mouth while eating. "We are going to make that right chief. Looking at Marcus, blinking, forever fast."

"Oh yeah, we go make that brother Man."

"That's what I'm talking about; you can bet that. Mark gives Marcu's dap. That's the Marcus I'm talking about."

I came straight home from school to days straight. I did nothing after school. No activities. I had just taken out the trash. I was walking back in on my way to my room. My mother and father were watching television. As the 5 o'clock news began, the newscaster Michael O'Brien, we start the evening news off with a tragic murder in Griffin Park. Police detective Louis Knight reported there was a body found by the lake. The victim Identity is still unknown. The victim was strangled and also suffered multiple stab wounds to the neck and back area. She was wearing a lime green and dark blue jogging suit. The suspect is still at large, if you have any information about this crime, please call crime stoppers at 1-312 victims, your identity will remain anonymous. They both looked back at Marcus at the same time. Marcus stood there in disbelief.

"Wow, I told Y'all, I told y'all I saw that I know, I know I wasn't crazy!"

"Now I know, son, that can't be a coincidence. Hell no, hell

34

no. What the hell is going on?"

"I have no idea." Standing with a stoic look on this face.

"Paul everything this Boy told us; he just repeated it verbatim. Two days later."

"Oh no, this is not the fucking twilight zone. Excuse my French; this shit is making me very nervous and scared. Honey."

"Baby, I don't think that you should be running in the morning, not until they find the killer that's still out there."

"Honey, you're right; I'll just do the treadmill in the garage." Sitting in the chair, with her head down, and hand over her face.

"Dad, do you think I can see into the future."

"How the hell, do I know, son! I can't even wrap my mind around what I just heard on the TV. Five minutes ago. You reading the future, is the farthest thing on my mind right now."

The telephone rang it was a Detective Henderson

"Good afternoon, I'm trying to reach a Mr. Davis."

"Speaking, May I ask who's calling."

"Yes sir, his is detective Henderson, one of our officers came by your house. A couple of days ago, to speak with your son Marcus. I'm doing a follow-up.

"Do you think that there's any way I could come by and have another talk with your son Marcus? I'm sure he might have some more information after seeing the news about the murder."

Mr. Davis replied, "Certainly, Detective Henderson. We would be happy to have you come over and speak with Marcus again. Please come by whenever you're available."

Detective Henderson thanked Mr. Davis and informed him that he would be heading over shortly. Mr. Davis hung up the phone and turned to Marcus, who was still in shock from the news report.

"Marcus, Detective Henderson wants to speak with you again. He'll be coming over soon. Are you feeling up to answering more questions?" Mr. Davis asked with concern. Marcus nodded slowly, trying to process everything that had been happening.

"Yeah, Dad. I'll talk to Detective Henderson. Maybe he can help make sense of all this." As they waited for Detective Henderson's arrival, Mrs. Davis offered Marcus some comforting words. "Marcus, we're here for you, no matter what. We'll figure this out together."

A short while later, Detective Henderson arrived at their doorstep. Mr. Davis welcomed him inside, and they all gathered in the living room. Detective Henderson greeted Marcus with a kind smile.

"Marcus, I appreciate you agreeing to talk to me again. I know this is difficult, but it's important to gather as much information as possible. Can you share anything new that you might remember after hearing about the murder at the park?" Detective Henderson asked, his voice filled with empathy.

Marcus took a deep breath, trying to recall any additional details. "I... I can't remember anything new, Detective. The dream I had was vivid, but it still doesn't make sense to me. How could I have seen all that?"

Detective Henderson listened attentively, nodding his

understanding.

"We're trying to piece this puzzle together, Marcus. Sometimes, things may not make sense immediately, but we'll keep investigating. It's possible that your dream could hold some significance, but we'll need to explore all avenues."

Marcus felt relieved that Detective Henderson wasn't dismissing his experiences. He began to share more about his dreams, hoping that it might lead to some answers.

As they continued their conversation, the Davis family knew that they were not alone in this troubling situation. With Detective Henderson's support and their unwavering support for Marcus, they were determined to find out the truth and bring justice to the victim and her family.

Together, they would navigate the confusion and uncertainties, inching closer to the answers that seemed elusive. In the face of the unknown, they would rely on their strength as a family and the dedication of the authorities to uncover the truth.

"Marcus, I need you to come straight home from school tomorrow. Detective Henderson is coming over to talk with you again at 4 o'clock."

"Okay, dad, no problem. I'm going to take a walk around to Mark's house if that's okay."

"Go right ahead, son. Just make sure you stay safe and avoid the streetlights catching you."

"Okay, Pops." I hurried upstairs to grab my camera. As I walked off the front porch, I ran into Mark who was also heading towards Griffin Park.

"Marcus Davis, where are we headed, man?" Mark asked,

looking up at the sky.

"Griffin Park, no doubt," I replied, camera in hand. Mark noticed the camera and suggested we go to the other side near the football fields, where we could freely capture moments without anyone bothering us. Excitedly, Mark grabbed my arm, getting in my face, and said, "Let's get it. Let's go to Griffin Park!"

We arrived at the park, where a concrete bridge with metal railings stood over a tunnel known as the Echo tunnel. Walking through, we made various noises, listening to the echoes. The graffiti inside the tunnel fascinated us with its unique art. We noticed a strong police presence due to a recent body found in the park, leading us to be more cautious. Before the tunnel, we passed a beautiful circular water display, shooting streams of water up into the air. On the right side, there was a statue of a man on a horse, which intrigued me. I promised myself to research the history behind it later. As darkness approached, we decided to head back home before the streetlights turned on. But as we made our way through the park, I heard a plea from somewhere behind us.

"Please, don't do this to me."

I looked around but saw nothing. The voice repeated, and it seemed to be coming from behind us. Curious, I looked through my camera's viewfinder and noticed lights by the tunnel on the bridge. As I directed my gaze towards the tunnel, my heart skipped a beat. A man wearing a gray hoodie held a knife to another man's throat. I couldn't see his face, but I started recording what was happening.

"Mark, did you see that?" I asked, feeling a mix of fear and confusion.

"No, I didn't see anything! What are you talking about?"

Mark replied, looking around anxiously. Realizing that only I witnessed the horrifying scene, I felt a sense of urgency to escape. We ran as fast as we could, screaming and catching the attention of a police officer on horseback.

"What's all the commotion about, boys?" the officer asked.

"I just saw a man get his throat cut and hung off the bridge," I gasped. The officer urged us to go home while he hurried to the scene. We ran until we were too tired to continue, finally stopping at my house. Mark and I entered, our hearts pounding.

Mr. Davis asked what was wrong, seeing our terrified faces. I blurted out, "I saw a guy get murdered at the park!"

Mark denied seeing anything, pacing nervously. I handed My father my camera, convinced that it had captured the evidence, but he found nothing on it. Mark and I were shocked as I could clearly see the video while my father and Mark's couldn't. Confused, we concluded that only I could perceive what was happening, unable to explain why. Mark decided not to go home, fearing for his safety, and we all walked him home together.

As rain started to fall, Mrs. Davis arrived, and my parents agreed to drive Mark home. During the car ride, I zoned out, lost in my thoughts, pondering why nobody could see the footage on my camera. It felt like I was questioning my own sanity.

Upon reaching home, I asked my parents about a statue I saw near the bridge in Griffin Park, but they were unaware of its history. This piqued their curiosity, and they suggested I research it. With my mind still reeling from witnessing another murder, I excused myself to my computer to look up information on the statue.

While engrossed in my research, Tonya, a girl from a neighboring house, called me to come over. I slipped out and made my way to her beautiful brick house with a charming porch swing and vibrant flowers in the yard. We spent time together, and Tonya confessed her feelings for me. I was pleasantly surprised to discover how much we had in common, and we agreed to explore a relationship. the popular girl that everyone admired, and I couldn't help but feel lucky to have her in my life. As the night wore on, I just couldn't shake off the events of the day. The fact that no one else could see what I captured on camera troubled me deeply. I shared my concerns with Tonya, who listened attentively and offered her support. We spent the rest of the evening enjoying each other's company, temporarily forgetting about the horrors of the park.

That night, with unanswered questions and a confusing mix of emotions, I headed back home

I went to the back door to find my dad in the kitchen, cooking himself a meal.

"Son, were you upstairs sleeping or studying?" he asked.

"No, I went over to Tonya Jenkins's house," I replied.

"I can tell there's something on your mind. Share with me, son," he said, sensing my hesitation shrugged my shoulders. "It's nothing much, really."

"Nothing much, really? I can see that smile on your face. Is Tonya your girlfriend?" he asked, smiling himself.

"Yeah, dad, she is," I admitted, unable to contain my excitement.

"I knew it! Tonya is a beautiful girl, Marcus," my dad said, smiling even more.

"I can't wait to tell your mom. Honey, come in here!" he called out.

"Oh, my goodness," I interrupted, placing my finger to my lips to signal my dad to keep it a secret.

"Do you not want your mother to know?" he whispered.

"No, not really," I replied, hoping to delay the news reaching her.

At that moment, my mom walked into the kitchen.

"What's going on, honey? Hey Marcus, I thought you were upstairs," my mom greeted us.

"So did I, but guess what," my dad chimed in, glancing at me. "He actually went to Tonya Jenkins's house."

My mom covered her mouth in excitement.

"Oh my God, my baby is growing up! I'm so happy," she exclaimed.

"You know what? I'm going upstairs. Good night, guys," I said, feeling a mix of embarrassment and amusement.

"Boy, looks like I have to buy you some condoms now," my dad teased.

"Honey, leave him alone," my mom interjected, trying not to laugh.

I couldn't help but burst out laughing. My mom and dad were truly one of a kind. They always had my best interests at heart. I couldn't wait to share the news with my friend Mark -

I knew he would be thrilled for me.

"I'm going upstairs to catch the 10 o'clock news."

Hoping for any updates on the murder in Griffin Park. As I sat in front of the TV, I couldn't help but wonder why the camera footage remained unseen by others. My mind wandered, contemplating the mysteries unfolding within Griffin Park and the strange occurrences I had witnessed.

The Rundown

A thought crossed my mind about the elderly chess players in the park. Mr. Wilson must be around 90 years old, and I remember Mr. Tom mentioning he was 87 the last time I watched them play. If anyone knows about Mr. Hemmingbird and the camera factory, it would be them. The park had a designated area off the corner of Decatur and 110th St., with ten beautifully detailed chess tables integrated into the design. Mr. Wilson and Tom were fixtures there, and you could always count on their presence. Mr. Wilson lived right across the street from the park, so he had a perfect view of the chess tables from his front porch. He stood at 5'10", weighing 225 pounds with a substantial belly, a bald and dark-complexioned head, a large nose, gray eyebrows, and a thick gray mustache. Old Soul, his chess buddy, had hair around the sides and the back but was bald on top. He constantly wore a hat and was known for his stories, some of which suggested he had been a pimp in the past. He stood tall at 6'2" and weighed 230 pounds, with brown skin, a prominent forehead, a thin mustache, small eyes, a small nose, big ears, and a fondness for food.

On the chessboard, they were formidable opponents. However, as I sat in front of my computer, my mind began to drift, and I found myself dozing off. I decided to get up from my chair and walk to the bathroom to freshen up and contemplate what was happening to me. I sat on the edge of my bed with a swirl of thoughts racing through my mind, absentmindedly rubbing my right palm across the top of my head. I eventually laid back and stared blankly at the ceiling.

Suddenly, I could hear voices echoing in my mind, as if from a vivid dream.

"Please don't do this to me."

"Hey, what are you doing, come on, Mark, let's get this guy."

The man bolted away, running through a tunnel, while I realized that my legs seemed to be moving rapidly, as if in pursuit. But despite the speed of my legs, I felt like I was going nowhere. Mark yelled out in the distance,

"Marcus, I almost had him."

As Mark reached out to grab the man, the assailant swung a large knife, narrowly missing Mark's arm.

"Man, he almost cut my arm off!" Mark exclaimed.

In response, I shouted, "Hit him high, and I'll hit him low."

"You'll never get me," the attacker scoffed.

I lunged at him from behind, wrestling him to the ground as he tried to stab me with his knife. I managed to pin his left hand, clutching the knife, to the ground. Struggling to see his face, I heard him taunt, "You can't see me because you don't want to see me, Marcus." Suddenly, he broke free and fled, knife still in hand. I noticed a whirlwind forming, swiftly spinning in a circle. Thousands of faces appeared before me, their eyes closed, pleading for my help, all while flashbacks of a clock-topped factory flooded my mind. Mark's voice broke through, urging me to be vigilant.

"Marcus, lookout."

I caught a glimpse of a man wearing a gray hoodie, forcefully pushing me, and that's when I started falling, screaming for help.

"Help, help, help!" I woke up in a state of panic, still screaming and covered in sweat. My dad entered my room, standing at the door, observing me as I lay in bed.

"Marcus, it's time to get up. You're going to be late for school. Do you need any help getting up?"

"No, I'm good. Sorry about all the commotion, Dad. That dream felt so real," I replied, trying to shake off the lingering fear.

I made my way downstairs, grabbed a banana and an apple, and quickly informed my mom that I was off to school. She questioned my choice of breakfast but didn't press further as I explained that I needed to meet Mark at our usual corner. Indeed, Mark was waiting for me as I arrived at our designated spot on the way to school.

"Guess whose house I went to last night," I gleefully shared.

"Whose house?" Mark replied curiously.

"Tonya Jenkins'," I revealed, savoring the surprise in Mark's reaction.

"What? Seriously, man, stop messing around."

"Nah, man. I'm telling you the truth. I asked her last night," I answered, blinking rapidly and stuttering slightly in my excitement.

"No way, Marcus! Did you make a move?"

"I won't disclose all the details, but I did kiss her," I coyly responded.

"No way!"

"You're damn lucky, Marcus. Congratulations! She'll be great for you," Mark exclaimed joyously.

"Thanks, man. That means a lot, especially coming from you."

"Oh, by the way, Mark, do you think those old heads over by the chess table play chess this early in the morning?"

"There's no telling with them. They're always out there, no matter the time of day or night. If the sun is setting, they're playing. If the sun is rising, you can bet they're there too! Marcus, I think it would be better for us to swing by after school. That way, you won't be rushed, and we can have a proper conversation with both of them. You know they'll be there after we get out of school," Mark suggested.

Both of us attended Carver High School, and my dad always emphasized the importance of investing our efforts during our high school years. I made sure to focus on my studies, although it was easy to get distracted by the allure of beautiful girls surrounding us every day. Carver High had no white students; the only white individuals we encountered were our teachers. In fact, I now realize that there were just five white teachers in the entire school. It took a certain degree of boldness for them to teach at Carver High. But Mark and I referred to it as

"Blackness at its best" and I truly cherished the experience. Whenever I contemplated deviating from the path my dad had encouraged, I could hear his voice guiding me.

"Son, this is your only opportunity for a free education, so make the most of it."

I don't know why, but that particular day seemed unusually long at school. I kept my eyes glued to the clock, barely hearing a word the teacher said. I was itching to leave so I could hear what the old heads had to say about Mr. Hemmingbird and the camera factory. Patience wasn't my strong suit, and as the final period dragged on, I found myself unable to stop my legs from shaking anxiously. It felt as though the clock had frozen, time moving at an agonizingly slow pace. But when the bell finally rang, it was as if a weight had been lifted. Mark and I met at our usual spot after school.

"What's up, man?" I greeted him.

"Not much," Mark replied.

"We still going to talk to the old heads, right?"

"Oh, definitely. Let's head over there."

As we arrived at the park, we found the old heads engaged in their usual banter and trash talk. Mark stood on one side of the chessboard, and I stood on the other, hands in my pocket. The weather was perfect at a pleasant 78 degrees, ideal for any outdoor activity. The ten chess tables were situated within a walking track encircling the park. People could be seen playing chess at all hours of the day.

"Hello, how are you all today?" I greeted them cheerfully.

Old Soul glanced up at me and responded, "It sounds more like 'how are you doing?' rather than a simple greeting."

We all shared a laugh, and Old Soul crossed his arms, covering his mouth.

"You could decipher all that from the sound of my voice?"

I chuckled.

Old Soul exclaimed, "Please! It's not about that. Usually, you guys are all like 'yo, yo,

yo, what's up!'"

Mr. Wilson joined in the laughter, adding, "He got you there, young blood. So, what's on your mind? Wait a second, can't you see I have a crucial move to make? Give me a moment, he's about to make a grave mistake, and I'm going to teach him a lesson."

Mr. Wilson spoke softly to himself, "That's a check," before executing the move deliberately. "Checkmate, Mr. Postman. You're done."

"Come on, man, you only pulled that off because the youngsters are here. I was deep into your territory."

"Yeah, sure," Mr. Wilson responded, raising his hand to silence Old Soul.

Old Soul laughed heartily and said, "You're just too disrespectful."

"Now, tell me what's on your minds," Mr. Wilson inquired, his attention focused on me. I smiled, positioning my left arm across my stomach with my right arm resting on top, hand under my chin.

"What do you guys know about Mr. Hemmingbird? You know, the statue in the park. And do you have any insights or information on why the camera factory was burned down in the early 1900s?

Mr. Wilson pulled his glasses down to the end of his nose, tilting his head slightly forward as wrinkles appeared on his forehead.

"Son, that was eons ago. I was still a little boy," he said.

"Shit, young blood," Old Soul replied. "I can remember what I had for breakfast this morning, let alone the 1900s."

"I bet you can remember the ass-whipping I just gave you," Mr. Wilson said, looking at Old Soul with wide eyes.

"You know my sister May; she's a hundred and seven. Sharp as a tack, she remembers everything. She's right there on the other side of the park, where people toss those flying discs."

"You mean Frisbees?" Mark asked.

Mr. Wilson looked at Mark, nodding. "Yes, that's the name of those things. You're bright, son. Stay in school."

Mr. Wilson pointed his finger towards Mark. "Yeah, that's it, what he said. Now, there's a house directly on the corner of Patrick. It's 2869 Patrick."

"There's an old lady always sitting on the porch over there," I said to him.

"That's my sister. Don't y'all go walking up to her house, she'll shoot you. You guys still want to stop by today?"

"Yes, sir, I would like to," Marcus replied.

"Well, let me call her first." Mr. Wilson pulled out his cell phone and dialed his sister's number.

"Mae, girl, what are you doing right now?" Mr. Wilson spoke into the phone as I listened. I couldn't help but think how country he sounded.

"I've got two youngsters over here by the chessboard,

nice young men. They want to know if they could stop by your house to ask you a couple of questions about some history. You know, you never forget anything. Hell, I can't even remember why I called you," he said, chuckling.

"Boy, you need to stop. That's fine with me. Send them on around here," Mae replied.

"Okay, Mae. Right now, I've got to finish beating up on Old Soul," Mr. Wilson said. We walked over to Miss Mae's house. Mark was looking down, hands in his pockets, shaking his head.

"Man, I hope she's not mean. You know some old people can be mean as hell."

"Come on, bro, think about it. If she was mean, do you think she would let us come over?"

"Hell yeah."

"And why is that?"

"So she can get her mean streak on for today."

"Man, if you don't shut your dumb ass up! I am going to tell her what you said. With your frail

blinking ass. Man, you've pissed me off!"

"Come on now, man, don't do that," Mark said, blinking continuously.

"Okay, okay, I'm sorry. But you heard him say she'll shoot you."

"Come on, man. This is Chicago, what do you expect?"

"Not that, and you can bet that. your ass is on one!"

Mark and I walked up to Miss Mae's house. She was sitting on her porch in a rocking chair, a long gray Afro framing her brown-skinned face. She was 5'5" tall and 115 pounds, with light green eyes and a very soothing voice. Her small nose highlighted her features, and she still had all her teeth. She lived in a small, 1,200 square-foot dark brown brick house with eight stairs and hand railings on both sides. The front door had a white screen door on it, and there was a big glass window with an awning over it on the left. A row of bushes started from the end of the house, leading up to the stairs. Rosebushes on the right side made the house look pleasant. Miss Mae lived alone but had two daughters and one son who checked on her every day. Sitting on the porch, observing the activities in the park across the street, was a daily routine for her. She called it "people watching" as she rocked back and forth in her dark brown rocking chair, on top of which she kept a snub-nose nickel plated black handle 38 special.

"You must be the two young fellows that my brother sent over," Miss Mae said, turning her chair to face us.

"Yes, ma'am," I replied loudly. "My name is Marcus, and this is Mark."

"You don't have to speak so loud; I can hear just fine," Miss Mae said with a smile.

"Oh, I'm sorry. How should we address you?" I asked.

"Miss Mae is fine. Can I offer you young men a soda or a glass of water?"

"No, thank you, Miss Mae. I'm okay. What about you, Mark?"

"No, I'm good too," Mark replied.

"So, what did Bill say you wanted to talk to me about?"

Miss Mae asked.

"Okay, Miss Mae," I said as I put my backpack down next to my leg on the porch.

"I was doing some research on the statue in the park, Mr. Hemmingbird. I wanted to know if you knew anything about why people burned down his factory back then."

"Oh, my goodness. That was so long ago. If I'm not mistaken, my mom, Betty Ann, told me that Mr. Hemmingbird had four children. One of them was mentally challenged and a bit off, if you know what I mean. That must have been about 90 years ago. His name was Fred, I think. People back then, including my mom, used to say that if you mess with Fred, you'll be dead. A lot of rumors circulated that he was a killer. One incident my mom told me about was when Fred was with a girl in the marketplace. She was related to the Morgans, a wealthy family at the time. Everyone had seen them together there. The next day, she was found dead in the lake on the factory property. It was just a lake back then. That was the last time she was seen alive, and Fred was the last person seen with her. The Morgans suspected he had something to do with their daughter's death, but they couldn't prove it. Rumors were that the Morgans burned down the factory and maybe even killed Fred. His death was..."

"Suspicious, no one knew how he died."

I smiled. "Wow! Miss Mae," I exclaimed. Mark blinked rapidly, taking a deep breath. "You are amazing to be able to remember all that from so long ago."

"The Hemmingbirds' parents made sure their children didn't want for anything. But you see, if you give a child everything, they will not appreciate anything. Now, that boy Fred, I wasn't the first person he attacked. There was a lady who got a job at the factory. I can't recall her name right now, but it was oh Paula Ann. She was one of those Creole girls. My mom was the only one who paid attention to how Fred looked at her. It was eerie and creepy. One day, my mom saw Fred talking to Paula Ann outside by the Rose Garden. Paula Ann never showed up for work again. The next day, her people came by asking if she had come to work. Now that I think about it, my mom told me Henry Hemmingbird knew his son was a little unstable. Come to think of it, give me a second, you boys wait here." Miss Mae got up from her rocking chair and went inside her house. She returned with an old, restored photo. It had seven people in it - her mom and her friends who had taken the photo while working at the factory. I pointed to a girl on the left of Miss Mae's mom and said, "That's Paula Ann." Miss Mae confirmed,

"Yes, it is." Mark smiled and said, " What! Is that your mom, Miss Mae, right there?" Miss Mae replied, "Yes, it is." Mark chuckled, "

Look at her, Miss Mae! Oh, she was not playing back then!"

Miss Mae's beautiful smile lit up. "Don't you start nothing with me, young fella," she laughed. "Those were good times back then!"

"Well, Miss Mae, it's been exceptionally well talking with you. I greatly appreciate everything today, but I've got to go. I was told to come straight home from school," I said.

"Well, better get a move on, young man."

"Okay, even though Mark thought you were going to be mean. And Mr. Wilson said you were going to shoot us," Mark laughed.

"What's wrong with these guys?" I said, looking at Miss Mae. "I don't know what you're talking about," Mark

53

defended himself, turning to look at me, still blinking and smiling.

"Does this face look like it would treat somebody mean? No, ma'am."

"Well, if you boys ever want to come back and visit, you're more than welcome,"

Miss Mae invited us with a smiling face. She found it so funny that she couldn't stop laughing, holding her side. We decided to go through the park. There was a jogging track with big trees forming an arc over it, blocking out the sunlight. Most people would walk when reaching that area of the park. There was a vendor selling hot dogs, lemonade, pretzels, and nachos with cheese right where the shade trees began. The trees stretched for at least 150 yards. It was so peaceful, though occasionally there would be homeless people around in that part of the park. As Mark and I reached the entrance by the trees, we hadn't noticed an old homeless man. We were having a conversation about what Miss Mae had told us about the Hemmingbirds when the man approached us.

"Could you buy me a hot dog?" he asked, rubbing his hands together.

"What the hell! Where did you come from?" Mark exclaimed in surprise.

"I would like a hot dog, please, please," the homeless man pleaded with wide-open eyes. The man's face was covered in marks and bruises. He smelled horrible, his teeth were rotten and yellow, his hair was gray and matted, and his clothing was dirty and raggedy. He seemed to be in pain, hunching over as if his back hurt. He wore a long, dirty black trench coat. His voice was creepy and scary, and his appearance suggested he hadn't bathed in months. He mumbled continuously under his breath, and the dirt under his fingernails was unbelievable. Standing there, he pressed all ten fingers against his lips. The stench of alcohol and urine surrounded him. He had two solar panels, one on the front and one on the back, each measuring 2 feet by 2 feet, plugged together. The hot dog vendor became upset and started yelling at him to leave.

"Get away from here! I said, get away from here! Goddamn it, I'm going to call the police. You're scaring off my customers!"

The homeless man started backing away and walked off to lay by one of the trees. I then ordered a hot dog, and Mark and I continued walking in the direction the homeless man had gone. When we reached the area where he had been lying down, Marcus stood over him and handed him the hot dog, saying, "Here you go, sir," in a kind voice. The man, with his mouth full, bit into the hot dog and started devouring it as if he hadn't eaten in months. Suddenly, he yelled out, "I heard you talking about the Hemmingbirds. Nothing is going to come to you but death!" He continued shouting, "Death!" and started running off, though not very fast due to his age.

"Nothing but death!"

Mark and I stood there, looking at him as he ran. Mark turned to me and said, "What the fuck was that about? He just came out from behind the tree, scaring the shit out of me, man. You can bet that, shit."

"I don't know, but I've seen that homeless man here in the park before," I replied. By the time Mark and I finished our twenty-five-minute walk through the park and up the street, my dad was standing on the porch with Detective Henderson. When I walked up to the house, my dad immediately confronted me. "What's going on? I told you to come straight home from school."

"I know, Dad, I forgot," I admitted.

"Forgot? I don't want to hear that. You're wasting my time and Detective Henderson's time. You know, I should charge you $50 for not being on time," my dad scolded me, emphasizing his belief in punctuality.

"I apologize to both of you for not being on time," I said, looking at my father and then at Detective Henderson.

"That's not acceptable. It doesn't even sound sincere. Get in the house," my dad

replied, shaking his head in disappointment.

"We'll talk about this later," he added. We all walked into the movie room. My dad and Detective Henderson took seats next to each other, and I sat in my dad's favorite chair against the left wall. It felt like an interrogation room, although I had never been in one. If I had to imagine, I would think it would feel like this, making me feel small as if I had shrunk five inches.

"Good afternoon, Marcus. Let's start with everything you remember that day, about what you saw. Take it step-by-step and try your best not to leave anything out, if possible," Detective Henderson began. I recounted the story, then he asked, "Do you still have that camera, Marcus?"

"Yes, sir, of course," I replied.

"Is there any way I could check it out?"

"Sure, let me run upstairs and grab it," I said.

I inserted the old flash card back into the camera, then came back downstairs and handed it to Detective Henderson. He examined it closely and asked, "Did you take the flash card out of the camera?"

"No, sir, it's the same flash card," I responded.

"I don't see anything on it. Did you happen to erase it by accident?" the detective inquired.

"No, I did not. The video is right there on the camera," I explained, feeling confused.

"I don't see it!" Detective Henderson raised his voice and hunched his shoulders with an attitude.

"I see it!" I interjected, looking offended. "Marcus, what the hell is wrong with you? Show some damn respect!" My dad scolded me.

I stood there, looking down with my hands and feet together. "Dad, I didn't do anything," I said in a low voice.

"You look at the officer when he is talking to you!" my dad demanded.

"Yes, sir," I replied.

"So, Marcus, I'll ask you again. Did you happen to erase the video that was on here? Because I don't see anything," Detective Henderson pressed.

"No, sir, I did not," I insisted.

"Is there any way I could take this camera down to the lab and bring it back to you tomorrow? I want to see if we can retrieve the video," Detective Henderson requested.

My eyebrows shot up in surprise, and I glanced at My dad, who seemed to be leaving the decision up to me.

"No, I don't think so. I need my camera for a photo shoot

tomorrow," I replied confidently.

The officer looked at Mr. Davis for confirmation, and he nodded. "That's not my decision. It's his camera, it's his choice," Mr. Davis affirmed.

"Listen, Marcus, you and your father have provided valuable information regarding the two murders you witnessed. This camera could be crucial to our investigation. I could obtain a warrant and forcefully take it from you, but I don't want to do that. Instead, I'll give you a couple of days to think about it. If you change your mind, call me, and I'll come back to pick up the camera. I'll get back to you as soon as possible, I promise. I have high praise for you from your father, and I trust you'll do the right thing to help this investigation. Mr. Davis, Marcus, have a good day," Officer Henderson said before walking out of the house.

"Son, what's been going on with you? Talk to me. Why were you late getting here?" my dad asked, concerned.

"The truth," I replied simply.

"Yes, son, please, tell me the truth," he urged.

"I was doing some research on the statue. Mark and I stopped by the park to talk to the guys who play chess there. They're known as the old heads. I thought they might have some information. Sorry, Dad," I confessed.

"Okay, son, but next time, use your cell phone. Call me. That's what it's for. In fact, where is your phone? It's probably not even charged. It's probably upstairs on your dresser," my dad raised his eyebrows, subtly scolding me.

"You never carry it with you. And what's so important about this statue in the park?"

"Well, he's got a camera on his shoulder, and I brought my camera. I just wanted to know why he's so special that he has a statue in such a huge park," I explained.

"Okay, son, now I understand. But why didn't you tell me that instead of not calling, not checking in, not doing anything? Two murders have occurred nearby. I need to know where you are at all times. Is that clear, Marcus?" my dad emphasized.

"Yes, Sir," I replied, acknowledging his concerns.

My dad grabbed me by the back of my head, pulling me close for a firm hug. "I love you, son, and I'll do everything I can to protect you. That's all I want. I couldn't live with myself if anything happened to you."

"Dad, do you think I did the right thing by not giving him my camera?" I asked, seeking his opinion.

My dad put his hands up under his armpits and stood there, looking at me thoughtfully. "I have no idea. Maybe the camera isn't finished with you yet," he smiled. "You are the creator of your reality; perhaps that's why you're the only one who can see what's on that camera."

I was taken aback by his profound response. "Wow, Dad, I never thought about it like that. Can I please be dismissed? I want to go upstairs and do some research on the computer."

"Yeah, go ahead," my dad granted, encouraging me to pursue my curiosity.

The Investigation

I went straight to Google and YouTube, which are my best friends when it comes to research. I was surprised to find very little information about Hemmingbird in Chicago. But then I stumbled upon something intriguing. In 1895, I discovered that there was a man named Henry Hemmingbird who lived in a magnificent mansion in Chicago. The mansion was a three-story, 18,000-squarefoot beauty situated on a 5-acre lot. The bricks used for the construction were imported from Austria and had a lovely light gray color. As you approached the mansion, you would encounter nine concrete steps leading up to a wide front porch adorned with two large round pillars. Inside, the mansion boasted nine bedrooms, nine bathrooms, a vast library, and nine fireplaces.

The floors were a stunning combination of wood and Spanish marble. The white vaulted ceilings trimmed with cherry oak wood added a breathtaking touch throughout the mansion. The large chandeliers in the living room and dining room shone with perfection, complementing the sunlight streaming in through the ample windows. Upon entering the front door, one couldn't help but be amazed at the open space. The first thing that caught your eye was a grand white staircase trimmed with cherry oak wood that extended 50 feet from the front door. To the left, there was a spacious coat closet, while the right-side wall curved elegantly towards a beautiful cherry oak wood archway. This archway showcased the history of the Hemmingbird family through generations of photos, revealing snapshots of the family's journey, including the factory, former employees, business partners, and photographs of Henry's run for office. To the right of the staircase stood a stunning oval-shaped library. As you stepped inside, it took a moment for your eyes to adjust to the uniqueness of the space. The room was adorned with custom-made bookshelves that extended from floor to ceiling all around the room. A railing located at the top and bottom of the bookshelves was attached to a ladder, allowing easy access to any book in the library. It was a treasure trove of literature, housing thousands of books. Burgundy suede chairs were placed throughout the room, emphasizing the richness and sophistication of the space. A solid dark brown oak desk stood in front of a window, draped with dark blue curtains held open by gold ropes adorned with blue tassels.

The library's large windows provided a splendid view of the estate. As you moved through the hallway behind the staircase, you would encounter a long, wide passageway running from one side of the house to the other. Three luxurious rooms faced the back of the staircase. In the center room, a majestic painting of Henry Hemmingbird himself hung proudly over the fireplace. Adjacent to the painting was a valuable black baby grand piano placed on a large black stable platform. The keys were barely visible from the angle at which you entered the room. This piano was a family heirloom that had been cherished for generations. It had been used by three generations of granddaughters to practice their recitals. In the corner on the left side of the fireplace, you would find a round table adorned with a brass flower vase imported from Egypt. The vase was always filled with an assortment of flowers that added vibrancy and life to the room. The cherry oak wood wall against the white walls enhanced the overall look and feel of the room. Large chandeliers illuminated the space, creating a warm and inviting ambiance. The far-right room of the mansion was a captivating cigar room. The centerpiece of the room was a large, colorful Persian rug placed in the middle. On either end of the rug were two dark brown, soft-cushioned leather chairs, accompanied by smokeless ashtray-tables. Plush, dark brown leather extra-long sofas adorned the other sides of the room. On the far-left side, there was a fantastic movie theater. Two massive cherry oakwood doors welcomed you into the room, while low, dim lights guided you toward the center of the floor. A small concession stand with popcorn and candy awaited to the immediate left as you entered the room. The theater had a seating capacity of 18 people, and dark purple drapes surrounded the space, providing an authentic movie theater experience. Moving upstairs, you would encounter five remarkable bedrooms.

The outside terrace, overlooking the city, felt straight out of a movie. The basement accommodated a sauna, steam room, and jacuzzi, providing a perfect space to relax and unwind. The Hemmingbird estate had been put into a trust by Henry Hemmingbird, who was well-versed in the laws and intricacies of estate planning. All of Henry's descendants, including children, grandchildren, and great-grandchildren, were welcome to enjoy the estate for special holidays and family gatherings. However, none of the family members actually lived in the mansion full time. They found it to be too big and opulent for everyday living. The Hemmingbird family was incredibly wealthy, with what people referred to as "old money." Their wealth stemmed from real estate and stock market investments. They had a dedicated staff that took care of the estate, ensuring its impeccable maintenance. All family members agreed to preserve the estate exactly as Henry had designed it. Now, let's shift our focus to Tyrus Hemmingbird, the grandson of George Hemmingbird and the great-great-grandson of Henry Hemmingbird. Tyrus was born in 1983 and graduated from Yale University with a master's degree in economics. He lived a life of luxury as a trust baby, enjoying the privileges that came with being part of old money. Tyrus was a divorced father, raising his son named Ryan. He stood at 5'10", weighing 178 pounds, with dark brown hair, a pointed nose, and piercing blue eyes. Tyrus took pleasure in various activities, with hunting being one of his favorite sports. His passion for hunting had begun at a young age, as his father, George, had given him his first gun when he was only 12 years old. Tyrus had embarked on hunting expeditions around the world, specifically targeting big game with his trusty bow and arrow. He resided in the high-prestige neighborhood of Lincoln Park and drove around in his preferred cars, a brand-new Maserati and Ferrari. One distinct feature of Tyrus was a long scar he had under his left jawline.

One day, while Ryan, Tyrus' four-year-old son, was taking piano lessons, he noticed something peculiar. As he ran to his father after the lesson, he couldn't help but spot a button hidden under the fireplace mantle. It was a button that could not be seen by someone standing up; it was only visible from a lower vantage point, like that of a child or someone lying on the floor. Intrigued, Ryan pointed out the button to Tyrus, who then hushed him and made a promise to keep it a secret. They shared a playful moment, with Ryan agreeing to keep the secret safe. After bidding his son goodbye, Tyrus made his way back to the estate. There, he was greeted by James, the loyal butler who had been taking care of the Hemmingbird estate for the past 50 years. James, standing at 6'2" and weighing 180 pounds, had a distinguished presence with his gray hair, light brown eyes, thin nose, and lips. He was also a second-degree black belt martial artist. Tyrus informed James that he had some personal matters to attend to and generously offered him the rest of the day off. James, grateful for the unexpected time off, mentioned that Martha, his wife, and he would be attending their granddaughter's first recital. She played the flute. Tyrus congratulated James on this exciting event and asked him to convey his greetings to Martha.

With the formalities taken care of, James's bid Tyrus farewell and went on his way. Tyrus, feeling a surge of anticipation, made his way to the hidden room behind the staircase. As he passed by the piano, his heartbeat quickened, excited about the mystery connected to the button he had discovered. He reached the fireplace and pressed the button, hoping for some sort of revelation. To his surprise, the platform on which the piano sat started moving forward. He walked closer, and as he realized it was a staircase leading to a hidden room in the basement, his awe grew. The space was dusty and untouched for quite some time. Tyrus descended the stairs, his mind filled with curiosity, wondering what this place could be. The scene was dark and somewhat eerie, as if nobody had set foot in this part of the estate for years.

Tyrus stood at the bottom of the stairs, peering into the darkness, and couldn't help but exclaim, "What the hell is this place?" The room was poorly illuminated by an old bulb. He paused, absorbing the atmosphere, and continued his exploration. Hanging from the ceiling was a chain, from which Tyrus pulled to turn on a dim yellow bulb. The bare bulb swung back and forth on a long cord. As Tyrus entered the room, the first thing he noticed was an old wooden desk positioned about 10 feet from the stairs. In front of the desk, there sat a brown wooden chair that appeared as though someone had just stood up from it a century ago. It felt like stepping into a time tunnel.

The room spanned 220 ft and featured a bathroom to the left of the wooden desk. Everything inside was aged, the remnants of bygone eras. In the right corner of the room, there stood a small closet with spiderwebs covering its door. On the right wall, there was a neatly made-up bed with a single pillow. Dust had settled for centuries and decades, preserving an immaculate, albeit antiquated, atmosphere.

Tyrus began exploring, coming across a collection of old

photos that belonged to his great-great-grandfather, Fred Hemmingbird. Fred stood at 5'10" and had a pronounced limp from falling off a horse at the tender age of seven. He possessed a strong English accent, a bald head with a comb-over hairstyle concealing his bald spot. His forehead was sizable, and he wore round glasses with thick lenses. His slightly yellowed teeth, thick dark eyebrows, and brown eyes completed his distinctive appearance.

Inside the closet, Tyrus discovered a brown trench coat with pockets specially designed to carry knives. This revealed Fred's past as a two-time knife-throwing champion. At the bottom of the staircase, there was a button that closed the platform, sealing off the secret room from the inside.

Tyrus stumbled upon an old diary on a shelf in the closet, which explained the reason behind his father Henry's creation of the secret room. Henry had built it as a hiding place in case the family faced any threats in his absence or during business trips. The entry dated November 8, 1889, offered intriguing insights into Fred's history.

There was a young girl, Paula Ann, who worked at the factory. Whenever she looked at me, it felt as if she was passing judgment. I couldn't stand the way she looked at me, so one night, I decided to close the gate to the factory earlier than usual. It happened to be a Saturday night, and Paula Ann was working late, unaware that the gate was shut. As she approached the front, I silently approached her from behind. stabbing her in the kidneys, and neck. She smelled so good! As I cut her throat, I watched the blood running down her neck. As her pulse began to slow down. I carried her body over by the lake, I laid her body in the position with both arms and hands, covering her vagina. With her dress halfway pulled up, showing legs thighs, I began ejaculating over her corpse. I ripped her dress off, disposing of her body into the lake. and then burning her dress in the factory's fireplace. Tyrus was standing there reading some dark, demonic, sick, shit. Fred was a volatile killer. His diary told the dark side of his great, great grandfather.

The more Tyrus started to read, the more he started to see himself. Between the pages, it talked about the troubles Fred had. anger issues, the voices he heard. Fred was killing rats, cats, dogs, and birds. He loved it all; it made him feel so good! The more the urge came, the more Fred wanted to hunt people. The thrill of getting caught excited him with a pleasure that he could not explain. Tyrus went out of the basement, taking the diary to read more. The more Tyrus read, the more his mind began to speak to him, about evil acts. Deep inside, Tyrus's thoughts began to take over His urge, he wanted to know how it felt when someone was taking their last breath. His great, great grandfather said the first time he killed; he felt as if his heart, was jumping out of my chest. Leaving my body from the rush that he felt. After it was over he wanted to feel it more; it was like an addiction. And. the only thing that could get him through it was more killing. Some of his stories were amazing; the places where he killed people were all around the factory. Besides, one lady Betty Moore. He killed her at the marketplace, down in an alley behind an old magic shop. Then he took her body to the lake. She had told him that he could never have her. The more the diary, Tyrus read the more of the fire began to ignite inside of him. He felt as if his great, great, grandfather was sitting there telling him the stories, of how to kill. Tyrus thought to himself, I would love to kill that ex-wife of mine, Jennifer.

"That was unlike Tyrus," he thought to himself, reflecting on his typically reticent and sneaky nature. Tyrus pondered the fact that Jennifer always seemed to be running over at Griffin Park, where the factory used to be. He couldn't help but feel that her presence was unnecessary in his and Ryan's lives; after all, his family was already big enough and supportive enough to take care of their needs. In Fred's diary, he detailed how he would meticulously study and follow his victims for days, sometimes even weeks, before taking action.

Fast forward two months. Tyrus found himself on his way to Griffin Park when a blue Honda Accord, with license plates reading "boogie man," stopped in front of him at a traffic light. "I like that," Tyrus said to himself, amused by the coincidence. He repeated it out loud, feeling a sense of excitement building within him. It was as if Tyrus was mentally preparing himself for a jog in Griffin Park, where he had spent the past two weeks observing Jennifer and familiarizing himself with her routine. Clad in a gray hoodie, he stretched near the trees and bushes next to the lake, hidden from the view of anyone outside. Although the area beyond the trees was open and exposed, behind them was a secluded spot. As Jennifer jogged by, Tyrus called out to her,

"Hey, Jennifer! How's it going? What brings you to this part of town? I didn't know you ran here."

Curious, Jennifer slowed down and looked toward Tyrus, recognizing his familiar face. As she walked up the gentle slope towards him, her guard remained down, as she had never perceived Tyrus as a threat before.

"Hello, Tyrus. What are you doing here?" she asked, genuinely puzzled by his presence.

"I was getting ready" at that moment. She was in striking range, by the trees and bushes. Tyrus struck her in the face, breaking her nose with a heavy blow.

"What the fuck is your problem." He then got behind her, putting a white rope around her neck. She's holding her nose, trying to stop the blood from running out.

"What are you doing." as he began choking her with the rope, she tries screaming out

"Help me; help me!" With both of our hands, trying to grab anything she could on him. As he continued squeezing the rope around her neck, Grinding his teeth.

"Shut up, you bitch! Shut up!" In a deep horrifying voice. Her body falls to the ground, and her leg starts to shake. Pulling his knife out from inside of his jacket, he started stabbing her body, grunting with rage, grinding his teeth constantly together. He stood over her body, with an insane look on his face, staring. With his hair out of place. Looking like a mad man. From the struggle that just happened. A devilish grin came across his face. Breathing heavily.

"That's from my great, great grandfather, bitch, with compliments from the boogie man." Looking around to see if anyone had been watching, He then carved in capital letters BM in her skin, on her back-left shoulder, with his knife. Cutting a patch of hair from her head, then dragging her body to the lake. Walking off through the park in a calm, relaxed manner as if nothing happened.

Tyrus was getting ready to get into his car. When an overweight white gentleman is walking by with his small Chihuahua, on a leash. He saw blood dripping from Tyrus right arm, he approached

"Excuse me; sir, is everything okay, you're bleeding."

"Yes, I cut myself on that swing, everything's fine. Are you from around here?"

"Yes, sir, that's my house right there on the corner," pointing his finger at his home.

"Oh, okay, Mr." Tyrus pause, "I didn't get your name."

"Barry Sanders, not any kin to the famous football player Barry Sanders. He's a black guy." With a small nonchalant laugh.

Two days later, Tyrus came back to the park, thinking Mr. Sanders would problem talk to the police. He could take that chance. He parked across from his house, waiting six hours. Mr. Sanders finally came out, after the sun had gone down. Doing his daily Routine. As he approached the park Tyrus, came up from behind him with a pistol in his hand.

"Don't look at me; just keep walking." He walked him over to the bridge.

"Why are you doing this to me." Pushing his gun in his back.

"Shut up and be quiet, keep moving, and put this got dame rope around your neck."

"Please, I don't want to die." Trying to turn and look back at Tyrus.

"Shut up; if you turn around one more time, I'm going to shoot you in the back of you got dame head," walking behind him, Towards the park bridge.

"Please, Mr. Please." Crying and weeping. Tyrus tied the white rope to the railing on the bridge. Now put your legs on the other side of the fence, Tyrus stood behind him Ripping his shirt open, carving BM in his back. Barry cried out

"Please stop!"

Tyrus, cutting his throat and pushed him off the bridge.

"Shut up. You rat bastard."

He picks up the Chihuahua dog, Stabbing the dog multiple time, laughing out loud. As he takes off jogging through the park.

Two days later, after he had killed his ex-wife. The Chicago Police Department contacted Tyrus. Detective Henderson contacted Tyrus to inform him about his ex-wife's untimely demise. It was Thursday morning at 10 a.m., and Tyrus was at his estate, spending more time in what he referred to as his secret room that remained unknown to others. The police department arrived at Hemmingbird's place but faced various obstacles while trying to reach the front door. It took them a frustrating fifteen minutes to overcome security and finally reach their destination. Detective Smith couldn't help but remark, "We shouldn't have to go through all of this just to ring a bell." After ringing the doorbell, Henderson, with his hands in his pockets, surveyed his surroundings. James eventually opened the door and greeted them, saying,

"Top of the morning, gentlemen. How may I help you?"

"We're looking for Tyrus Hemmingbird. This is his last known address," Detective Henderson explained, flashing his badge in front of James.

"I see, Sir," James replied, bowing his head slightly and gesturing to follow him.

"Please step this way."

Henderson and Smith entered the front door, both impressed with what they saw. Smith whispered, "Wow, this is quite the place."

While the detectives waited, Tyrus emerged from the basement where he had been working out. He walked up with a towel around his neck, wearing a white T-shirt and gray sweats, looking somewhat confused. "Hello, gentlemen," he greeted them.

"How can I help you?"

Henderson pulled out his badge and stated, "I'm Detective Henderson, and this is my partner, Detective Smith. Is there

71

somewhere we could talk in private for a moment?"

Perplexed, Tyrus asked, "What is this about?"

"Sure, right this way," Tyrus said, leading the detectives toward the library and occasionally glancing back at them.

"What did you say your names were again?" Asked Tyrus.

"Henderson and Smith, sir," Smith replied.

"Would you gentlemen care for anything to drink?" Tyrus offered, walking over to a small bar in the library.

"No, sir, not on duty," Smith declined. Tyrus took a seat at the long oak table, and the detectives joined him.

"Now, tell me, what is this all about?" Inquired Tyrus.

Henderson looked directly at Tyrus and asked, "Do you know Jennifer Hemmingbird?"

"Of course, she's, my ex-wife. We have a son named Ryan together," Tyrus responded.

Henderson continued, "When was the last time you saw her?"

"Well, she dropped Ryan off for piano lessons on Sunday. I waved at her from the

car, and that was it. What's going on? Why all the questions?" Tyrus questioned, increasingly perplexed.

"She was found murdered at Griffin Park on Sunday," stated Henderson as he observed Tyrus closely.

"What? Did you say!" Tyrus exclaimed angrily, his face growing stern. He closed his eyes, took a deep breath, and lowered his head.

"Murdered! How? Who was responsible?" asked Tyrus desperately.

"Griffin Park, according to our sources," Smith replied.

"What the hell was she doing there? And where is my son?" Tyrus shouted, calling out to James as he entered the room. "Could you please grab my cell phone from the workout room downstairs and bring the car around?" Tyrus demanded, his anger and distress evident.

"What's going on? What happened?" James inquired.

"That's what we're trying to find out, Mr. Hemmingbird," Henderson explained while standing up. He spoke with animated gestures. "Now, I know this is a bad time, but I have to ask: where were you on Tuesday evening?"

"Are you insinuating that I had something to do with this?" Tyrus replied, an alarming look on his face, staring at Detective Henderson, Tyrus raised both of his hands out to his sides and said, "No sir, but I have to ask, is this just procedure? Look Mr. Hemmingbird, I'm not the bad guy here. I'm on your side, just trying to get to the bottom of what happened. I'm just doing my job."

"I was here with Ryan; he had piano lessons," Tyrus explained as James returned with his cell phone and had already pulled the car around.

"James, could you please do me a favor and tell Detective Henderson where I was on Tuesday evening?" Tyrus requested.

"Why, Tuesday evening is Ryan's piano practice. You were sitting in the room, telling him he needs to do better on his transitions. Is there a problem, sir?" James asked, looking at

Henderson and Smith inquisitively.

"Yes, they just told me they found Jennifer dead," Tyrus informed them, shocked by the news.

"My goodness, Sir, my deepest condolences. Will there be anything else, Sir? I'll be waiting in the car. Good day, gentlemen," James expressed sympathetically.

Pacing back and forth, Tyrus spoke to Detective Smith, "I don't know how I'm going to tell my son that his mother is dead. How do you do something like that? Is there anything else that you officers require from me? If not, I need to find out where my son is."

"No, sir, that'll be all for now," Detective Henderson replied, walking over to Mr. Hemmingbird and looking him in the eyes.

"You know, I've been in the department for 25 years. Whoever did this, you can best believe I will catch them," Henderson assured Tyrus, extending his hand and shaking Tyrus's hand firmly.

"We'll be in touch, Mr. Hemmingbird," Henderson said as Tyrus walked the detectives back to the front door.

"Gentlemen, please keep me informed about what's going on, and thank you. Have a nice day," Tyrus requested before closing the door.

Tyrus already knew that his son was at his aunt's house, her sister on his mother's side. Having grown tired of talking to the detectives, he watched as Smith and Henderson walked back to the car.

"So, what do you think, Smith? Do you think Tyrus had something to do with his wife's murder?" Henderson asked.

"I don't know, Henderson; I really couldn't read him," Smith responded thoughtfully. They both got into the car.

"What about you?" Henderson inquired

"You know, everything comes out in the wash."

"True, but he got a solid alibi."

"For now, let's head back to the station and check if we have received any paperwork regarding the insurance policy. We need to uncover the motivation behind this incident."

Tyrus had reassured James that he could return the card. He had already spoken to Ryan's aunt, and everything was under control. They entered the room where the piano was located, and Tyrus instructed James not to disturb him, locking the door. Meanwhile, the family feline, Jasmine, gracefully wandered around the room. Tyrus pressed a button, revealing a secret compartment. He carefully picked up his most cherished knife, a genuine Gurkha Kukri, playfully swishing and slicing through the air. He adored the unique curve of its blade. With a composed demeanor, he took deep breaths, preparing for what was to come.

"Tyrus said in a low voice. I can't wait to feel the thrill of life, leaving someone's body again."

Talking to himself, he started swinging the knife slicing his arm on purpose as blood is dripping on the concrete floor; the sight of blood excited him. Making his heart race. He sat down on the bed in the room looking at the blood drops. The dust on the floor was so thick he never noticed the five-pointed pentagram star with the goat inside of it with a circle around the outside. The evil of his great, great grandfather ran deep. When the family cat came down in the room, he grabbed the cat lowly stroking its fur; the cat Jasmine has been a part of the family five years.

He sat at the desk, with the cat in his lap stroking the cat grabbing his knife. His eyes open up more prominently, his heart speeds up, biting his bottom lip taking deep breaths pulling back. Jasmine was just about to meet her death when she made a big cat scream scratching his leg, jumping out of his lap, running up the staircase out of the room. After he had been sitting there staring at the floor. Tyrus decided to wipe his blood up, grabbing a large towel cleaning all the dust off of the sizable 5-foot symbol painted on the floor. He didn't know what the artwork on the floor was about or what it meant, so he started searching the web from his smart phone. Looking for one thing, but finding himself looking at something different, the human body, and the 20 significant arteries and capillaries in the body. He wanted to be a better killer than his great, great grandfather ever was.

He ordered a life-size male realistic, flexible manikin. To practice his killing techniques on. Also, fake blood he ordered, somehow, he wanted to put it inside of the dummy, to see it run down and out after he had done his stabbing and cutting. He was Practicing being a vicious obsessed killer. That's all he thought about after killing his ex-wife. After wrapping his womb on his left arm, he came out of the secret room. Just at the right time, his sister knocked on the door because it was locked.

"Tyrus, it's me, Victoria, open up."

He walked over to open the door. Hello there, giving his sister Victoria the impression that he had been sitting at the piano.

"I came right over after I heard the news; I went by your house you weren't there." Hugging him, "I'm so sorry, are you okay."

 "I guess Tyrus said I don't know what to feel."

"Well, I just want you to know that I'm here for you whatever you need I'm here, do you understand me."

Victoria was 5 feet 10 inches, blonde hair, a hundred and 135 pounds, light brown eyes, thin lips, medium nose, sweet cheek with dimples; she wore contact lenses. Her makeup always looked flawless, she kept herself in good shape, she had been playing volleyball in high school, college, now in a volleyball league she had two children. Kevin, Nancy.

"What happened to your arm?"

" He told her he accidentally cut it trying to pull Jasmine out of the tree."

"Where is my nephew Ryan at. Is he getting bigger? How are you going to tell him about his mom?"

He looked over at her sticking his eyebrows straight up in the air and shaking his head.

"I don't know."

"What's going on with you Tyrus, it seems like you have the weight of the world on your shoulders. At this moment. That's not like you, I mean I'm saying you guys weren't even together, I know you feel bad because it's Ryan's mother. But you had no control of this. nobody knew that this was going to happen."

"James, Victoria and I are going to sit upon the terrace, could you bring me a cappuccino?"

"Yes, sir, and what would you like my beautiful lady, you're looking so lovely?"

"Oh James, stop you're always boosting my confidence, could you bring me a glass of port, if we still have some.

Sandman would be great."

They walked up the stairs turning to the right towards the Terrace when they stepped outside on the roof of the Terrace was like a big greenhouse. The frame was Cherry Oakwood, with the entire roof made out of glass. The right wall was a retractable glass that opened up to bring in the fresh air. There was a large flower planter going all the way across the front of the Terrace. It was 6 feet high; the flowers were in bloom with the sweet scent of nature. There was a barbecue grill in the left corner on the outside of the retractable glass. A small glass table set in the middle of the room with four chairs surrounding it. There was a fireplace on the left wall, with a big brown cushion leather sofa that surrounded it. The sun had gone behind the clouds; the rain started coming down; it was nice and cozy. With the outside fire going, the smell of the storm, the sound of the city in the background, they both walked over and sat at the table.

"Let me ask you a question Victoria, I was driving the other day, and this car pulled up next to me there was a five-pointed star with a goat head in the middle with a circle around the outside do you have any idea what that means."

"You know I remember there was a girlfriend of mine named Patty when I was in college. She said her father was part of an evil organization that sacrificed people she'd never seen it. She just had heard about it."

James walked in with their beverages

"Here you are, ma'am."

"You know ma'am makes me feel so old, James."

"I'm so sorry, lady Victoria," both of them smiling. James handed her a glass of wine

"Thank you, James. You are a lifesaver."

"And for you, sir," putting the cappuccino in front of Tyrus.

"So why did you ask me that"

"I had seen it on the side of the car. It's crazy that people advertise things like that, so you're telling me they actually have people that worship the devil?"

Victoria looked at him with a look on her face like you can't be serious.

"You didn't know that there are people like that?" Tyrus is sitting up with both elbows on the table with his cappuccino between his arms, with his hands together.

"I don't know about these types of things, that's why I'm asking."

"You know there was a rumor going around you probably were too young to remember, but they said that our great, great grandfather was part of a cult. You know killing people for power, sacrificing people that type thing; but I never believed it."

"What are you serious?" Tyrus looking at Victoria

"Yes."

"Wow, you're blowing my mind right now," laying back with his left hand on his four head. "That's unbelievable."

Deep in his mind, he wanted to tell her what he had found, but he couldn't. They continued talking when his oldest brother walked out onto the terrace.

"What's going on, good people."

His sister got up, walking over towards him, greeting him with a hug and a kiss on the cheek.

"Hi, John, it's so good to see you. When did you get in town?"

"Wow, look at you aren't you looking good. I got in last night."

Tyrus stood up, "How's it going, big bro."

"Man, I got here as fast as I could. I just heard what happened on the news this morning, so how are you holding up?"

"I'm good for right now, the police came by questioning me, but everything's fine."

"Look at you, big bro looking good. It looks like you put a few pounds on Donna's keeping you and the kids busy, eating well." John smiled

"Yeah, pretty much, so what's going on with you two guys what are you talking about."

"Old stuff nothing important" James walked out on the terrace good

"Afternoon, sir. Is there anything you would like?" With hesitation.

"No thanks to James I'm good I'm going to be meeting the wife in about 30 minutes for lunch."

"Very well, sir. Good day," James turned and walked off.

"Man, it's good to see you guys, what has it been three weeks." Putting his arms across Tyrus and Victoria's shoulders.

"You know we need to start being more committed to hanging out with one another. Our sons and daughters need to see each other more?"

Tyrus, nodding his head, "you're right, big bro, you're always right."

"I agree, Victoria reply smiling, so how's the business going. "Tyrus pulls out the chair from the table,

"Have a seat."

"No, I'm good I've been sitting on that same plane for 6 hours. The last thing I want to do right now is to sit down. I'm going to be sitting down at the restaurant with Donna for at least two hours,"

Laughing out loud. The drugs are going excellent. It's going to be one of our most extensive quarters coming up. Which means excellent bonuses." Smile.

John ran the Hemmingbird's family-owned small pharmaceutical company, and a dispensary out of Colorado. Making the family millions, not including the real estate company that Victoria ran, that also brought the family millions of dollars.

She also ran her own research company for a product she developed called brain stem. John was 39 years old, 6'3" 240 pounds, dark black hair, muscular build, dark eyes strong. John was a man with distinct features. He had a brownish mustache and goatee, along with a full head of hair styled in a comb-over. His nose was of medium size, and he had well-defined lips. He typically dressed down in a polo shirt and blue jeans, complemented by his black Ray-Ban Bose sunglasses.

"Look, I've got to run; Donna should be here any minute. We're going to have sushi for lunch at her favorite spot downtown," said John, as he gave his brother a firm handshake and hug.

"You stay strong and take care of yourself. You already know that if you need anything, just pick up the phone. I love you, man," John added.

"I love you too, Bro," replied Tyrus.

Victoria approached, and John hugged her tightly, swinging her from side to side.

"I love you," he said.

Victoria patted and rubbed her brothers back affectionately. "I love you too," she said, planting a kiss on his cheek.

"As much as I'd love to stay, I better get going. I want to stop by the office before heading home. I'll catch you guys later. I'm staying here until Sunday, and I want to see both of you before I leave," John explained. Then the two of them sat back down at the table and continued their conversation.

"So, is there anything else you've heard about our family?" Tyrus asked Victoria.

"I remember mom telling me about how she once stumbled upon something strange in the basement. She saw eight men dressed in black tunics with hoods over their heads, forming a circle around a naked woman. She mentioned our great-great-grandfather, Fred, being involved in some secret society as a priest. Mom mentioned a hidden compartment in the basement that nobody has ever found. She talked about a wall with a painted tree," Victoria recounted.

"Really? No way!" Tyrus exclaimed.

"I remember it vividly because it scared me. Do you recall how we used to play hide and seek in the basement? That's why I never stay over here alone. It's too damn scary. I must have been around 10 or 11 when she told me that story. She said our family has a lot of secrets in its history. Anyway, I'd better get going. I want to stop by the office before heading home," said Victoria.

"Okay, Victoria. I appreciate you spending time with me. Let me walk you out,"

Tyrus offered. In his mind, Tyrus couldn't wait to go back to the secret room and continue searching for the hidden compartment mentioned by his sister. He thought to himself, "I've got to finish reading that diary." As Tyrus and Victoria made their way to the door, James and Annabella grabbed their jackets and headed out to get supplies and food for the estate.

"Will you be dining here again tonight, sir?" James asked.

"I haven't made up my mind yet," Tyrus replied.

"Very well, sir. Annabella and I will be gone for a couple of hours," James informed.

"Okay, that's fine, James. You guys take your time and hurry up!" Tyrus laughed.

"You know I'm just kidding. Take all the time you need," he added.

"Alright, Victoria, I'll be talking to you soon." Tyrus gave her a warm hug.

"You take care of yourself, and don't hesitate to reach out if you want to talk," Victoria said.

"I won't," Tyrus reassured her. With everyone gone,

Tyrus immediately headed for the piano room. He opened the secret passage and descended, searching for clues. He inspected trigger handles, buttons, anything that might reveal another hidden door. The room wasn't large, leaving limited places to conceal something. He moved the bed and checked behind the desk, in the bathroom, and the coat closet, but found nothing. However, when he removed a trench coat from the hook, he noticed that the hook had three parts shaped like a triangle. He pushed and pulled on the triangular sections, producing a faint snap. Behind him, the wall behind the door revealed a large crease extending from ceiling to floor. Opening it, Tyrus found a small hidden room inside the closet, covered in spiderwebs and dust. To access it, he had to close the closet door, which revealed a wall that folded in two pieces. Inside, the small hidden room measured 10 feet wide and 5 feet deep.

On the right wall hung a black tunic, accompanied by a pentagram necklace emblazoned with a charm. On the white wall in front of him, an ancient-looking oak tree was painted with black and gray hues. Numerous branches sprouted from it, breaking into 13 different families. In the bottom left corner, a small box containing various pieces of jewelry and a photo of disfigured victims lay. At the base of the tree was the name "Dracula Draconis Hemmingbird," representing three generations of grandfathers, leading back to Jack the Ripper Hemmingbird. As he examined his family chart displayed on the tree, Tyrus felt a sense of pride in being a Hemmingbird. He discovered that his great-great-grandfather had been involved in an organization with Hemmingbird Williams, Sanchez, Wolff, Abramowitz, Kozlowski, Vân Leeuwen, Romano, Beneventi, Dunn, Morrison. Tyrus was eager to return to my diary to see how everything connected, but he had left it in his car, a thick book with around 300 pages. He retrieved it and he started reading, the pieces of the puzzle began to fall into place. I stumbled upon detailed accounts of rituals and sacrifices, unraveling the reasons behind them. I settled into a cozy chair by the fireplace in the library, with a glass of wine in hand. I delved into its pages, transported to a time when the dining room table was set, and eight people gathered for dinner. Martha and Henry, Darlene, Doris and Charles, Ethel, Arthur, and Amos. Darlene's presence that evening was meant to meet Amos.

Flipping back to 1905, I learned that young Fred would often listen intently outside the dining room door, hidden behind a wall, as his father Henry entertained guests. And that fateful evening, as the conversation progressed, Darlene, Martha's sister, became intoxicated and began airing out their family's dirty laundry. She openly criticized Henry for his lack of respect towards Martha and suggested that Martha should leave him. In her drunken state, she even went as far as labeling Fred, Henry's son, as mentally disturbed and argued that he should be confined to a mental asylum.

With every word Darlene uttered about him and his family, Fred's rage intensified. Meanwhile, Martha, sitting at the table, fiercely defended her husband and assured everyone that there was nothing wrong with their son. Darlene's laughter echoed through the room, causing Henry immense embarrassment and shame. The dinner guests, a mixture of colleagues and politicians, were potential allies for Henry's political aspirations. Darlene, a ballerina, wore a necklace adorned with a gold ballerina pendant, while her skirt and shoes were made of elegant ivory.

As the guests bid their farewells and left for the night, Henry was still troubled by Darlene's behavior, repeatedly apologizing to his guests. Martha and Henry retired to their master suite. Once everyone was gone, Darlene and Amos found themselves on the front porch, swinging gently on a porch swing as they conversed. Little did they know, Fred had positioned himself beside the house, intently eavesdropping on their conversation. As they said their final goodbyes, Amos disappeared into the dark street, vanishing into the night, while Darlene remained standing on the porch... Fred emerged from behind her, taking her life in an instant, and her body vanished without a trace. Inside the secret panel, Tyrus noticed the jewelry nestled in the box. Killing Darlene had been deemed beneficial for his family. He believed that she could never again embarrass his father. For quite some time, people suspected Amos of involvement in Darlene's disappearance.

Fred went on to reveal that he always kept something as a memento from the people he killed. In 1912, Henry Hemmingbird ran for office against Frederick Walker III, who mysteriously met his demise during the political run. Walker had been outshining Henry, having graduated at the top of his class while Henry hadn't finished high school. Curiously, Mr. Walker drank tea before his wife did. Strangely enough, Henry emerged victorious in the election, becoming the mayor. Tyrus couldn't help but think, "If there's a way to get someone, Fred sure knows how to come up with it."

"I have to be more creative," Tyrus muttered to himself, pondering whether the network of influential families still existed and how he could contact them. He wondered if they had been admiring his work, oblivious to the fact that they had set themselves up for failure. Politics required a profound understanding of the people's needs—a mere ability to run a business didn't equate to running a city. Walker was far from a well-liked person.

Fred had closely followed the election, as his father was leading the polls. He wanted to ensure Henry's victory, so he took necessary measures for his father's success. Fred meticulously observed Walker's house from dusk till dawn for an entire week, strategizing ways to exploit him. One early morning, as the sun illuminated the horizon, Mrs. Walker placed tea on the back porch to brew under the sun's warmth. Fred silently approached the porch and subtly tipped over the jar, causing it to spill just enough to force her to make a fresh batch. With that done, Fred hastened home to retrieve a lethal poison, knowing it would be the end for Mr. Walker and anyone else who drank the tea.

Fred had become the family's designated killer, carrying out the Hemmingbird family's dark deeds. Not only for them, but also for 12 other families and constituents connected to his father. While his father never explicitly ordered him to commit these crimes, he would subtly hint at the need to address certain situations. Fred willingly embraced the role of the Hemmingbird family's executioner.

Everyone is Connected

I had it in mind that I would find the homeless man whom I had bought a hot dog for in the park. I wanted to learn what he knew about the Hemmingbirds. A week had passed, and I made plans to walk through the same area of the park near the concession stands, hoping to find him. As school let out, Mark and I took a leisurely stroll through the park, observing everyone who passed by. I mentioned to Mark that some people hide in plain sight. Equipped with a small pair of binoculars, we walked for 45 minutes before Mark spotted the homeless man rummaging through a trash can. The shine from the solar panels on the heel of the parking lot caught his attention. To reach the park, one had to descend 25 stairs with a silver handrail in the middle or traverse a steep grassy hill adjacent to the stairs. Mark and I approached the man as he continued picking through the trash.

"Excuse me, sir," I said, and he turned to look at us.

"Do you remember me from the hot dog stand? I brought you a hot dog last week," I said. He held an old piece of pizza from the trash in his hand.

"Yeah, what do you want?" he replied in a nasty and mean tone.

"You mentioned something about the Hemmingbirds

last week, and I wanted to ask you a couple of questions," I explained.

"About what?" He asked, with a repulsive smell emanating from him, and food remnants smeared on the side of his mouth.

"Let me buy you a couple of hot dogs and something to drink, and let's have a seat in the park for a minute, if you don't mind," I proposed. He dropped the old pizza on the ground, eying me suspiciously.

"You'd do that for me? Why? What do you want?" He questioned.

"I just want to talk, that's all," I reassured him before handing Mark $10 from my pocket.

"Could you please go down and buy two hot dogs and something to drink, along with a couple of bags of M&Ms for me?" I requested.

"Can I get some M&Ms too?" Mark asked.

"Sure, two bags of M&Ms for both of us," I confirmed, and Mark jogged off to the concession stand in the park.

"What's your name?" I asked Abe as we began walking down the stairs.

"Abe Huff," he responded.

"My name is Marcus," I introduced myself, and Abe suggested, "Seeing as your parents raised you well, you don't have to call me 'sir.' Just call me Abe."

"Okay, Abe."

By the time Mark returned with the food, Abe was already

seated at a picnic table. I sat on top of the table, while Mark leaned back against a nearby tree. Abe wore an old, raggedy blue-black beanie, a long, dark brown wool coat, gloves with no fingertips, torn tan-brown khakis with holes in the knees, and a pair of old steel-toe boots. The day had turned out beautifully, with the sun warming the park.

"So, what do you know about the Hemmingbird family?" I inquired.

"I used to work for them. I was a groundskeeper. That damn son of his was a crazy son of a bitch, I tell you. You had to watch your back around him. He was definitely a killer. Let me tell you something—I saw him kill a lady one evening, and I even know where he hid the weapon. And, you know what? I've held onto it all these years," Abe recounted with intensity.

"Get the hell out of here," Mark exclaimed, leaning over and resting both elbows on the table, blinking rapidly.

"What's wrong with your eyes? Is that some kind of disorder, the rapid blinking?" Abe asked Mark, curious about his behavior. While slurping the ketchup and mustard off his grimy fingertips, he finished devouring his first hot dog.

"Hell no, Abe," said Mark, glancing at me and shrugging his shoulders. "I just can't stop blinking.

"I burst into laughter. "What do you want me to say?"

"So, Abe, where's the knife?" I asked, my eyes lighting up.

"I'll tell you, soon as I'm done with this delicious Frank. Better yet, I'll show you. But you must promise never to tell anyone. If you do, I'll have nowhere to go," Abe cautioned.

Mark looked at Abe with a puzzled expression. "Why would you tell us about it then?"

"Because, for some reason, I have a good feeling about you guys. I trust you both, and I know you'll do the right thing and keep it a secret," Abe replied.

There was a hidden part of the park near the lake, an old bunker from the factory's past. It remained unknown to everyone, except Abe and the maintenance crew who cared for the park. The entrance was concealed by bushes of all shapes and sizes. To access it, one had to walk through a large bush that grew over the entryway, uncovering a small 3 x 3 feet metal hatch. Upon opening it, an eight-foot ladder led down 20 feet into a 15 feet wide hallway, eventually leading to an 800 square feet box-shaped concrete room. Abe had been living in this bunker for over 30 years. In the room, there was a bathroom to the right upon entering. Abe explained that when the factory was torn down, the water was never turned off. He connected his solar panels to the lamps for lighting, so he wasn't crazy; he used them to charge his panels. Impressive, I thought to myself, as Mark wandered around the room. There was a military cot for Abe to sleep on, adorned with three thick blankets. Mark turned on the flashlight on his phone and entered the bathroom. He noticed a small 2 x 2 panel in the top right corner.

"Hey, Abe, what's this panel for?" Mark asked, intrigued.

"What panel are you referring to?" Abe walked into the bathroom and looked up to where Mark was pointing.

"It looks like there's a red nozzle. Is it to turn on the water?" Mark explained. "I know because my father turned ours off last week when fixing a busted pipe."

Mark grabbed a black chair from the corner, stepped on it, and opened the panel. He turned the nozzle, and water came rushing out of the sink and tub with a rusty hue. The water had never been used inside the bunker.

"I told you!" Mark exclaimed, turning off the water. "Remember to turn it off when you're done so no one suspects you're down here. Otherwise, they'll think the park is just using extra water."

"So, you mean to tell me I can take a bath now?" We both nodded enthusiastically. As I leaned against the wall, I asked Abe, "Now, where is that weapon you were telling us about?"

Abe walked over to an old-looking suitcase, rummaged through it, and pulled out a blood-stained knife enclosed in a transparent plastic bag. The dried blood gave the blade a gritty appearance. Eagerly, I took out my cell phone and snapped a picture of the knife inside the bag.

"Abe, this is incredible! How long did you work for the Hemmingbirds?" I asked, fascinated.

Abe took a seat in front of Mark and me. He wiped his face with both hands and took a deep breath. Then, he looked me in the eyes and started sharing his story.

"I didn't always work for the Hemmingbirds. In fact, I used to be wealthy. I was a silent partner with Henry Hemmingbird, Fred Hemmingbird's father. One night, I approached Henry and told him what I had witnessed his son doing. I had invested a significant amount of money in their camera factory, and the returns hadn't started coming in yet. My wife, Betty, was furious with me for risking our savings on Henry's company. Seeking to recover some of my investments, I confronted Henry, but he claimed all the money was tied up in the product. I don't think Henry had anything to do with it, but his son Fred came after me one night. Knowing the extent of his son's capabilities, I pointed my gun at him, pressing it against his head. I looked him straight in the eyes and warned him that if he ever came near me again, I would blow his damn head off. The very next day, I went to Henry and informed him about the knife I had seen his son use and hide, and that I now had it in my possession. I made it clear that if anything happened to me or my family, that knife would end up on the sergeant's desk at the police department. Henry must have talked to his son because Fred never confronted or approached me again. Betty divorced me after 25 years of marriage. I lost everything I owned, and the factory eventually burned to the ground. All the investors, including me, lost their money. I ended up working for peanuts as a groundskeeper for Henry, who had also suffered significant financial losses. But after he became mayor, he managed to accumulate wealth, thanks to putting people in key positions with the assistance of his son, who ran a secret organization. I never managed to recover from my losses, which is how I ended up in this situation today."

We were left stunned by Abe's revelation, and all I could do was shake my head in disbelief.

"Damn, Abe, you've been through hell and back. I can only imagine how badly you wanted to kill that son of a bitch. I sure as hell would've done the same! And what about you, Marcus?" Mark asked, turning to me.

Leaning against the wall, arms crossed, I blinked and replied, "Man, you lose any sense of time down here. That's for sure!"

"Abe, Mark and I are planning to make a move soon. I'll bring a few things over tomorrow: soap, canned goods, and maybe some old clothes my dad wants to get rid of. I'm sure my parents won't mind since it's going to be a good cause."

"Thank you, Marcus. That's very kind of you and Mark. I truly appreciate everything you've done for me." Mark and Marcus began walking back to the ladder to climb out of the bunker.

Earlier, before we ascended, I asked Abe where exactly the factory used to sit. Abe, Mark, and I were inside the bunker, and Abe started explaining as he drew on the wall with a piece of chalk. I took a picture with my phone to capture the location of the factory, intending to return and photograph the empty space at a later date.

"Guys, when you reach the top of the ladder, make sure to peek your heads out to ensure nobody is around to spot you. Thank you for everything, and I'll see you soon," Abe advised.

"Okay, Abe," I replied as I went up first, cautiously looking outside.

"We're good to go; everything is clear. Peace out, Abe. Talk to you soon," I informed him. Mark gave him a fist bump and added, "I can't shake your hand, it's too dirty. Take care, chief!" And then ascended the ladder.

Abe smiled and said, "They won't be here later on after today, chief," with a big smile on his face. It struck me that time had flown by as Mark, and I had spent two hours in the bunker. As we made our way back across the park, I walked with my head down, and both hands in my pockets. Glancing over at Mark, I remarked, "Old Abe turned out to be a cool dude, man."

"He'll be even cooler once he takes a shower. You can bet on that, chief," Mark replied, and we shared a laugh.

"As you would say, you can bet on it. Boy, you're something else. Where did you get that saying from?" I asked, intrigued.

"From my uncle, Steve. He's getting some treatment at this new clinic off of 111th and State Street. You should come with me on Friday after school. We can take the bus," Mark suggested.

"Don't you want to go by yourself?" I inquired, noticing a concerned look on his face.

"Not really," Mark admitted, looking up. "No doubt, I'll first have to see if my mom or dad has anything planned after I get out of school. You know how they are."

"So, what do you think you'll do with the picture of the knife?" I asked, curious about his intentions.

"I'm not sure yet. Maybe it will come in handy later," Mark replied.

"You can bet on that," I said, agreeing with a smile.

Tyrus received a call from his older brother, John. John informed Tyrus that they would be donating a $300,000 check to the mayor for his new research facility. The mayor happened to be an old friend of their father. John and Victoria believed that Tyrus would be the perfect candidate to attend the dinner and donate the check on behalf of the family for future business prospects. Tyrus gladly accepted and asked John to send him all the details. Shortly after, John forwarded Tyrus the information about the mayor's dinner, which would take place on Saturday, February 9, 2019, at 7:00 PM. Tyrus knew that some of the most influential families in Chicago would be in attendance.

Upon arriving at the mansion, James walked over to take Tyrus' coat. "James, please keep Saturday evening open. I'll be attending the mayor's dinner. Could you also prepare the white Rose Royce? Thank you, James," Tyrus requested.

James nodded his head respectfully. "Consider it done, sir. Will that be all, Tyrus, sir?"

"Could you please bring me a cappuccino in the library?" Tyrus asked, feeling impatient.

Tyrus wanted to relive the thrill of the kill again, so he continued reading more of the diary, trying to memorize its contents verbatim. A couple of days earlier, Tyrus had received a life-sized mannequin for practicing his art of cutting and stabbing in a secret room. He aspired to surpass the skills of his family members from the past. When his brother mentioned the money, they would be donating, Tyrus had a wicked thought. Why pay $300,000 to an organization when his ancestors would have simply eliminated someone? With a sinister laugh and a smirk, he decided to plot accordingly.

On the night of the mayor's dinner, held at the St. Jane tower, a stunning hotel, Tyrus stepped out of the white Rose Royce chauffeured by James, who held an umbrella to shield them from the rain. Tyrus wore a dark blue two-piece Zegna suit, a white shirt, and no tie, with a white handkerchief. As James walked him to the hotel's entrance, Tyrus expressed his gratitude, saying, "Thank you, James, that's very kind of you."

"It's my job, sir," James replied. They stood together under the umbrella, and Tyrus instructed James to call him thirty minutes before his departure. Tyrus then grabbed a poster-sized blank check and made his way through the lobby, admiring the hotel's refreshing art decor. The magnificent conference room greeted him with its renovated beauty: nine hanging circular chandeliers, floor-to-ceiling mirrors on both sides, and 75 tables set with white tablecloths, accommodating six guests each. As he walked in, Tyrus couldn't help but appreciate the splendid ambiance of the room.

"The carpet was dark gray and black, adorned with a beautiful design. William went by his first name, Ed. He approached and shook my hand with a firm, confident grip."

"Good afternoon, Tyrus. My goodness, you've grown into such a handsome young man. You're looking vibrant these days," he said, looking directly into my eyes. "Thank you for coming."

"It's my pleasure, Mayor. I'm delighted to be here. Thank you for the invitation, and happy belated birthday, Mayor."

The mayor was wearing a dark brown suit with a brown tie and white shirt, accompanied by a white handkerchief. He stood at 6'2" and weighed 265 pounds, slightly overweight. His gray comb-over exuded confidence, and just last week, he celebrated his 72nd birthday. With a deep voice, light brown eyes, and gray eyebrows, he sported a full salt-and-pepper beard and mustache, complementing his broad nose and slightly chubby face.

There was another gentleman who approached the mayor. "Tyrus, this is my friend, Marco Sanchez."

"It's a pleasure to meet you, Mr. Sanchez." "Likewise, Mr...?" Marco paused slightly. "Hemmingbird, Tyrus."

Marco Sanchez was a slim 36-year-old. He donned a black tuxedo with a white shirt and black shoes. His dark black hair and deep brown eyes added to his handsome features, while his flawless skin and thin, clean-shaven mustache completed the look. Tyrus handed the mayor a large blank check.

"Why, Mr. Hemmingbird, there's no amount on this check."

"Oh, I'll be filling in the amount once I present it to you. Trust me, it will be a substantial sum." Tyrus smiled.

"Well, thank you so much, Mr. Hemmingbird. You know our families have a great history together."

When the mayor mentioned their families' history, a lightbulb went off in Tyrus' head. He realized that both the mayor and Sanchez shared last names, which he had noticed on the wall in the secret room. He couldn't believe he hadn't connected the dots earlier. Was it a mere coincidence, or was he right in the middle of something significant?

As the guests mingled before the dinner, Tyrus took the opportunity to gather information about some of the attendees. He started with Marco, who was standing alone.

"This is a lovely dinner that the mayor has put together here."

"Yes, it is. He has managed to attract many prominent and wealthy individuals from the Chicago area."

"So, how did you come to know the mayor, Marco?"

"Our families go way back. He was a good friend of my late father, and I've been fortunate to have him as a mentor. He's a very nice guy."

"Oh, that's interesting. The mayor was also good friends with my father."

Tyrus overheard delightful laughter behind him, coming through the entrance. He turned to see the most stunning woman entering the room. She wore a white evening dress that extended to her knees in the front and flowed below her calves in the back. Her curvaceous figure filled out the dress gracefully. The crisp pleats at the front of the dress moved harmoniously with her every step. Her white and black heels added fierceness to her stride.

"And who might that be?" Tyrus asked Marco.

Marco chuckled, raising his hand to wave at the woman. "That's my sister."

"I'm sorry, I meant no disrespect," Tyrus apologized, never taking his eyes off her.

His sister approached, greeting Marco with a kiss on the cheek. "Hello, baby brother. How are you looking so sharp?" She said, playfully grabbing his left cheek.

"Hello, Isabella," Marco smiled. "You're looking stunning. Let me introduce you to Mr. Hemmingbird."

"Good afternoon, Mrs. Sanchez," Tyrus greeted, extending his hand. He gently bowed his head and kissed the back of her hand.

"Please accept my most humble apologies, Mrs. Sanchez."
"I like him, Marco."

Isabella stood at 5'5" and weighed 125 pounds. Her long, dark black hair cascaded down her back. Her flawless makeup enhanced her perfectly arched eyebrows, red lipstick, and pearly white teeth, all of which left Tyrus speechless. As he looked at her lips, he tried to turn away but found himself unable to. She, too, was staring at him. Their gazes locked until a voice came over the microphone, snapping him out of his trance.

"Good evening, ladies and gentlemen. Excuse me, I have to go up on stage now."

Welcome to the NDRC (New Development Research Center). The speaker unveiled a 40 x 60 picture on an easel, showcasing how the research center would appear once completed. The logo featured a globe with 'NDRC' written above it, representing new disease testing. As the event continued, Tyrus and Isabella maintained their attention on each other, as if no one else existed.

Tyrus found himself on stage, unaware of what the guest speaker was saying. His focus remained solely on Isabella. Suddenly, he heard the crowd erupt into applause, realizing that the speech had concluded. He joined in the clapping, only then realizing that he had been called to the podium. Jumping up, he exclaimed, "Excuse me! I'm sorry, I was preoccupied. I didn't know it was my turn to speak," jokingly.

Tyrus sat on the stage alongside three other individuals who were also making donations to the mayor's facilities. He approached the podium.

"First, I would like to thank the mayor for inviting my lovely family to this thousand- dollar-a-plate dinner. I'm certain the food is delicious. My family will be donating a check for..."

Tyrus looked behind the chair where he had been sitting. "Could you please pass me that check?"

A young lady seated on stage handed him the blank check. "Mr. Mayor, could you please come up on stage? I would like you to hold one end of the check, please. Can someone else please hold the other end?"

The mayor glanced back and called out, "Mr. Foster, get up here!" Both men held the check.

"I should have had this prepared before. My apologies,"

Tyrus admitted. He started writing the amount on the check. "The Hemmingbirds will be donating the sum of..." he said while writing out the amount. "Three hundred thousand dollars."

The entire room rose to their feet, giving him and his family a standing ovation. The mayor stood proudly behind the check, expressing his gratitude and acknowledging Tyrus and his family's substantial donation. Tyrus returned to the podium and quipped, "Well, Mr. Mayor, with this amount, I hope my dinner is free."

The mayor chuckled. The Hemmingbird family had made the largest contribution of the night. As the dinner party continued, numerous individuals approached Tyrus, thanking him and his family for their generous donation to the research center. After all the contributors had spoken and the donations concluded, the mayor brought Tyrus over to introduce him to two other gentlemen.

"Tyrus, this is Dr. Clinton Patterson, who will be spearheading the research."

The 5'8" Dr. Patterson from Boston weighed 158 pounds and had brown hair, blue eyes, and a soft-spoken demeanor. His long, slim nose and thin lips were complemented by a goatee and gold round-framed glasses. He wore a slightly disheveled black tuxedo, having indulged in a few drinks during dinner.

"Thank you for such a generous donation, Mr. Hemmingbird," Dr. Patterson expressed his gratitude.
"You're welcome, Dr. Patterson." Tyrus tilted his head slightly. "So, what is it that... You research?" Tyrus asked.

"Well, we are trying to find new developments besides insulin shots for diabetes and new-age technology for high blood pressure, that kind of thing."

"But if people just work out, they could easily reverse those diseases, right, Dr.?"

"Yes, but some people just don't get it, so this new research should help them out a lot. Mr. Hemmingbird."

"Let me also introduce you to the director, Todd Forest." He was 5'10" tall, weighing 240 pounds, with a full red beard and mustache, light brown hair styled in a comb-over, very light freckles on his face, a medium nose, and a big smile with small teeth. Forest had a slight stutter in his speech but was shaking everyone's hands.

"It's good to meet you, Mr. Foster and Mr. Patterson."
Tyrus thought to himself, something about Mr. Foster made him feel uncomfortable, but he couldn't quite put his finger on it.

"Excuse me for a minute, gentlemen," Tyrus called James to let him know that he would be ready in 30 minutes. Tyrus had become uninterested in the event.

Tyrus walked outside the room where the dinner was taking place. Miss Sanchez saw him step outside and approached him seductively.

"Leaving so soon, Mr. Hemmingbird?" she asked.

"Unfortunately, yes. I have other matters to attend to," Tyrus replied.

Miss Sanchez opened her purse, pulled out a business card, and handed it to Tyrus. Tyrus looked down at the card and realized she was the CEO of one of the biggest communication companies in America.

"So, it's you. I never put two and two together. I've heard a lot about you in the business world," Tyrus said, his voice low and seductive.

"Well, I hope whatever you heard was good," Miss Sanchez replied in a similarly seductive tone.

Tyrus stood there speechless, unable to think of anything to say. She seemed to sense his reaction and smiled at him. He continued to gaze into her eyes, smiling and hunching his shoulders.

"I don't have a card," Tyrus said with a playful wink. They both laughed.

"Well, you have my info. Don't let it go to waste," Miss Sanchez said, with a flirtatious tone.

James walked into the lobby and spotted Tyrus from afar, nodding his head. "That's my driver. Can I offer you a lift anywhere?" James asked with a smile.

Leaning over to Tyrus' ear, Miss Sanchez spoke low, letting her lips touch his ear, "No, my driver is outside," she moaned at the end, bringing an even bigger smile to Tyrus' face as she looked him straight in the eyes. Tyrus moved in close to her and gave her a slight kiss on the cheek.

"You know, I could feel that down my spine to a certain stiff place," Tyrus murmured with his eyes closed. Opening them slowly, he said, "I will be in touch with you very soon," as he started walking towards the front door to exit the hotel. He looked back at Isabella, blew her a kiss, and thought to himself, "Any other time, I would have…" he chuckled to himself.

After recognizing some names on the wall, Tyrus couldn't wait to get back home to continue reading more of his great-great-grandfather's diary. He wanted to find out if there was something he was missing, a handshake, a code, a secret word, or anything.

James opened the back door of the limo, and Tyrus got in. "Did you enjoy your evening, sir?" James asked.

"Yes, James," Tyrus told him. "I met a nice woman, Isabella Sanchez," smiling.
"That's fantastic, sir. Is she the Isabella Sanchez, the CEO of…I can't recall the company at this present moment?" James replied.

"Yes, that's her. How do you know her?" Tyrus asked, with a confused look on his face.

"Oh, I don't know her personally. I was reading an article in Forbes magazine, and I remembered her name and the lovely photo they had of her. It was a great article they did on her," James explained, looking at Tyrus through the rearview mirror.

Tyrus nodded his head in the back seat, smiling. "The world is a small place, James."

"Can you please stop by the nearest Starbucks? I need a cappuccino," Tyrus requested.

"Yes, sir."

When Tyrus walked into Starbucks, he overheard a conversation between two women sitting at a nearby table. They were discussing the clinic that the mayor had been raising funds for, but one of the women claimed that it was a front, and no real research was being done. She said her uncle had died due to the false study conducted at the clinic.

"Excuse me, ladies," Tyrus said, unable to resist joining the conversation. "I couldn't help but hear your conversation. Where is this clinic located? By the way, my name is Tyrus, and I deal with issues like this."

"What are you, some kind of lawyer?" One of the women asked.

"No, not a lawyer. I provide evaluations that bring about change," Tyrus clarified.

"The clinic is located by the University, right outside of Hyde Park, if you must know," one of the women replied.

"That's the new clinic the mayor is supposed to be opening, right?" Tyrus asked.

"That clinic has been open," the woman said, stepping back with a strange look on her face.

"That's right, and his ass hasn't done shit! He said he would, and I voted for his no-good punk ass!" The other woman exclaimed, standing with her arms crossed, clearly upset.

Tyrus reached out to shake her hand. "Your name is?"

"My name is Karen, and this is my friend Lisa," she said.

Karen was 5'5" tall and weighed 125 pounds. She had a small Afro, beautiful dark skin, thick eyebrows, and a medium nose with a diamond stud on the right side. She wasn't wearing any makeup and had on blue jeans, a brown turtleneck sweater, and light brown suede boots.

"He's gotten so many donations for that clinic in the last two years, that shit should have been done. But you know what? He's been bullshitting all these people out of their money, and that clinic they have people in right now is a damn dump. They don't even clean the dialysis machines. My aunt and uncle died at that raggedy motherfucker. That clinic has to go," Karen said, tears running down her face. The Starbucks manager approached and asked her to lower her voice.

"I'm so sorry, I just got a little emotional," Karen apologized.

Her friend Lisa nodded sympathetically. They had both been going through the same issues with the clinic.

Lisa was a tall, pretty woman, standing at 6 feet and weighing 157 pounds. She had dreadlocks, smooth and silky-looking skin, beautiful full lips, and wore black oval-shaped glasses. Lisa sat at the table, writing and taking notes.

"I had no idea all of this was happening at that clinic," Lisa said.

"Of course, no one knows," Lisa replied, with a subtle smile on her face. "We've been trying to get something done about the mayor's fake clinic."

"Well, let me say this to both of you. I assure you that I will be speaking with the mayor ASAP. And let me reiterate,

I had no idea this kind of thing was happening. I just left a fundraiser for the clinic where my family has donated $300,000, and right now, I feel like a total idiot. This is preposterous, and I am very upset about it," Tyrus said, turning red with anger.

"What Karen said, are you serious?" Lisa asked, with a surprised look on her face. "What did you say your name was again?" Tyrus answered.

"Tyrus Hemmingbird," he replied, picking up his cappuccino.

Lisa slammed her pen on the table, stood up, and said, "Your family donated the land that Griffin Park sits on, right?"

"You're right, and my family is guilty," Tyrus replied angrily, but his expression changed in an instant.

"Trust me, ladies, I will be having a talk with the mayor first thing in the morning," Tyrus promised.

Lisa and Karen walked over to Tyrus, looking him in the face. "Lisa said, you deserve a group hug. Bring it in."

The three of them hugged, taking deep breaths. Tyrus laughed.

"That's cool. I like that," he said, with a big smile on his face. "You ladies smell so good. That was refreshing."

"Now, that's how the laws of attraction work. You never know how it's going to come," Lisa said, finishing her sentence.

"But it is going to come," Tyrus added, still smiling. "You

know, I would feel right if I didn't ask if you ladies need a ride anywhere?"

"No, Karen said, we don't. But what kind of ride do you have? You look expensive, around here donating that kind of money," Karen said, shaking her head.

Tyrus laughed. "I do."

They both walked over to the window to see Tyrus's car. Tyrus looked back and said, "I'm in that." Karen looked at him skeptically.

"Man, your not in that," she said, shaking her head.

Tyrus laughed. "You're right. I almost got you. But like I said, I will be talking with the mayor first thing in the morning. Good evening, ladies. Enjoy the rest of your stay here at Starbucks."

Tyrus walked out while Lisa and Karen stood at the window, waving at him. James got out of the Rolls-Royce, opening the door as Tyrus approached. Tyrus turned around, waved at Lisa and Karen standing at the Starbucks window with their hands up over their heads, both wearing big smiles. Tyrus thought to himself, "Not only am I going to visit the mayor, but I'm also going to visit the clinic. Somebody has to pay."

Early Monday morning, Tyrus woke up bright and early for his daily routine of weightlifting, exercising, running 2 miles, and reading a portion of his great-great- grandfather's diary. By the time he finished, it was 10 o'clock, and he headed to the clinic to check it out. He wanted to get a look at how things were done before going to see the mayor.

A visit From the Past

On Monday morning, around 6:00 AM, Mark and I were walking through the park. I decided to head towards the lake and take a picture of the space where the factory used to be. At that moment, Abe emerged from the bunker behind the bushes, and Mark called out his name.

The three of them met up in the area where Mark had witnessed the first murder. "So, Abe, can you show me where the factory was? I want to capture it in a picture," Mark asked eagerly.

Abe pointed in a direction and said, "Look over there. Do you see where the end of the parking lot stops at the top of the hill? We are standing at the bottom by the lake, looking up. Now, come over here to the right, where the archway of bushes begins. That's where the right side of the factory used to be."

"So, you're saying that the lake now occupies the site where the factory stood?" I inquired.

"Exactly," Abe confirmed, as they stood there gazing back and forth between the two points of reference.

I took several photos and then started filming the area, trying to visualize how the factory used to look. "Thank you so much, Abe."

Remembering that my parents had given me $10 for lunch, I reached into my pocket and handed three dollars to Abe. "I still haven't forgotten to bring you those extra clothes and soap, but my parents have kept me really busy. Hopefully, I can drop them off later today."

"Whenever you find time, it would be greatly appreciated," Abe replied gratefully.

"Wow, Chief," Mark exclaimed with a big smile. "You're looking very clean these days." They all burst into laughter.

"Oh, man," Abe chuckled, shaking his head with his eyes closed. "That water feels so good on my skin. I'm getting myself together."

"Indeed, you can bet that, Chief," I agreed. "But we should hurry to school."

Mark and I arrived at school, and he hurried off to his first-period class. Cameras and video cameras were not allowed on campus, so I stowed my camera in my backpack. With five minutes to spare before the bell rang, I took out the camera and started reviewing the photos I had just taken.

As I watched the video footage, I noticed that the factory only appeared in the video, almost like an illusion. My heart raced, and I began to sweat, feeling a sense of unease. I see a gruesome murder taking place, a man stabbing a woman. The blood started getting on the camera lens, I tried to wipe it off but couldn't, the man in the video then laid her body in a specific position, putting her hands over her vagina and then started ejaculating over her body. What the fuck is going. On scared out of his mind, the man walked out of the viewfinder, coming back looking directly into the camera. In a Deep English accent and a horrifying voice with the knife in his hand. He was stabbing at the camera lens and looking as if he's looking through a peephole.

"I see you looking at me little black Nigga boy!" With a sinister evil laugh.

I dropped the camera, but the strap was around my neck. I closed my eyes looking down, feeling for the off button. Scared than I have ever been in my entire life.

I yelled out.

"Oh, my fuckin god! What the hell is going on."

I didn't even think about going into class; I took off running as fast as he could back to the park looking for Abe. I could hear that evil laugh in my mind. Running, thinking, knowing if I showed anyone, they would not be able to see what I had just seen.

I made it back to the park. I saw Abe sitting under a tree, Abe had just finished eating some fruit. I ran up to him out of breath.

"Abe how did that guy, the one you told us about, was a killer look. I can't remember his name." Bent over, trying to catch my breath sweating.

"Slow down, Marcus, what's going on. You look like you have seen a ghost." Standing up straight with the hands-on

113

top of his head. Breathing very heavily. Laughing hysterically afraid!

"Who are you talking about, Fred Hemmingbird?" With his eyebrows pulled close together in a frown.

"Yeah, that's him!" Shaking his head back and forward.

"Man fuck," almost out of breath.

"Well, it's been so long ago, Marcus."

"Let me share with you what I observed earlier today. There was a gentleman with a bald head, sporting a comb-over to conceal a prominent bald spot-on top. His round glasses framed his dark eyes, and his forehead was quite sizable. He was dressed in a white shirt, the sleeves casually rolled up, and unfortunately had yellow teeth that didn't add to his appeal. He wore brown khaki pants with a noticeable buckle and had a slight limp as he walked."

"Coming back to my encounter with this individual, his name turned out to be Fred, or as I would creatively describe him - 'the motherfucking Fred, goddam!'"

"Marcus, I'm genuinely interested to hear what you have to say. Don't worry about sounding crazy; people have often labeled me the same throughout the years."

"During my earlier visit, while I was busy capturing photographs of everything, I caught sight of a peculiar factory. I can vividly describe it to you. Additionally, I also happened to cross paths with Fred Hemmingbird himself. Killing a woman. Over by the lake, I can't make this up, man. And I know it sounds crazy, but I'm telling you the truth."

Abe got up from lying back against the tree and started walking over to the park bench.

"Marcus, do you know what you're saying? Let me say this: Native American Indians didn't like to take pictures because they believed taking a picture could steal their soul. So, in your case, maybe the camera somehow connected to the past. Fred Hemmingbird, wow, I don't know why the devil would give that son of a bitch another chance. I'm just saying."

I was squatting down, catching my breath, while Abe was sitting on the park bench.

"I never thought about it like that, maybe it could be," I said with a confused look on my face.

"Anyway, Marcus," Abe pointed at me, "why aren't you in school?" "I'm scared of what I just saw. I don't know what to do."

"What does your heart tell you to do?" I laughed out loud. "Run like hell."

"Run where? Wake up, Marcus, you can't run from everything. Sometimes you have to face your fears."

I put my head down, going into deep thought about what Abe had just said. "You know what I'm afraid of, Marcus."

"What's that, old man?" I looked him right in the eyes.

"Dying down in that bunker, and no one finding me," he

said with a serious look on his face, then looked down at the ground.

"Well, you can stop worrying about that. I'll check on you."

"What about when you go off to school?"

"It will be Mark's turn to look in on you then."

"Oh, god no. He will definitely let me die," they both laughed.

Now that I realized that the camera was something special, it could see things in the past and the future. I wanted to know more about the murders that Abe and Miss Mae told me Fred Hemmingbird committed. Instead of going back to school that day, I ended up walking to the bus stop, passing by Ms. Mae's house. She happened to be sitting on the porch.

"Good morning, Mrs. Mae."

"Hi, Marcus! Is that you? I can't see that far, but I know your voice. Why aren't you at school, little boy?"

"I'm headed to the library. I have some research to do."
"Oh, okay, that's good."

"Miss Mae, let me ask you a question. What year do you think it was when that guy was killing people?"

"April 1907, I remember it like it was yesterday."

"Wow, okay, Miss Mae. I've got to run. Have a good day."

"You too, baby."

I caught the bus to 400 S. State Street to the Harold Washington Library. I wanted to do some research on the history of crime that was committed in the area of Griffin Park in the early 1900s. I don't even think Griffin Park was around back then, and I know Chicago couldn't have been the murder capital of the United States at that time. The library itself was one of the most beautiful buildings I had ever seen. I remembered being at the Harold Washington Library during a field trip back in elementary school. I went straight to the history section, searching for old articles stored on microfilm. I found the year 1907 and started reading.

There was one article in the Chicago Tribune, posted in big, bold black letters on the front page. The headline read, "Body Found in Lake Stabbed to Death, No Suspects in Custody." I started reading the article, and it went on to describe the gruesome details. A young lady in her early 20s found stabbed to death, next to the Hemmingbird's camera factory. It was the third body found in April; police say a serial killer might be responsible for the murders. The article went on warning the public to be aware when going out alone. Chief police Daniel Scott the third was outraged he promised the people that he would catch the killer or killers responsible for the brutal murders of all the young women that were found in the last two months.

Article 2 months later stated that the killer still has not been caught, but the victim's list continued to grow, and the police had no suspects in custody. I kept doing my research and ended up at the Harold Washington library. I didn't make it back to school that day, but I knew the weekend was coming up. For a brief moment, a thought came to mind that Mark had asked me to go down to the clinic to visit his sick uncle with him. I wasn't really keen on going, but I continued reading the articles and came across one that talked about the police having a suspect in custody named Fred Hemmingbird in connection with the murders of several women. However, two days later, another report stated that the charges had been dropped due to lack of evidence or proof. The investigation was still open, but Fred was no longer considered a suspect.

Meanwhile, I was at the library all day and got a call from Mark, asking why I wasn't at our regular spot after school. I explained what happened and mentioned that I should be back on that side of town in a couple of hours. We chatted briefly before I mentioned that I was still planning on going to the clinic with him, reluctantly, only because he asked me to. We joked around and agreed to catch up later.

As I continued my research, I discovered that the mayor had raised $2.9 million to establish the clinic. However, when I reached the clinic, I was disappointed to find that the building was in dire need of renovation. It seemed like the money hadn't been put to use, and there were a large number of people waiting outside. I couldn't believe that all of them could be sick. The place was crowded, and it seemed chaotic. I ran into Karen and Lisa from Starbucks, who were also surprised to see me there. Karen sensed my frustration, and we discussed how the clinic operated, including the fact that patients had to pay for treatment.

Feeling frustrated, I approached the counter and asked to see the supervisor, director, or doctor, but they were nowhere to be found. It was already 11:30 AM. I asked the lady behind the counter what time the clinic closed, and she told me it closed at 5 o'clock sharp. I decided to leave and planned to return at closing time. My plan was to confront the doctor and seek answers. My heart was pounding, and adrenaline rushed through me. Before heading to the mayor's office for an explanation, I took a moment to calm myself down. I called my brother John, who picked up right away. I shared my frustration with him, particularly about the money we donated to the clinic and how it seemed to be mismanaged. John reassured me not to worry about it and that our family name would be fine. He suggested I stay away from political matters and trust him to handle everything.

Relieved, I thanked him and planned to get back to him soon. I realized that the mayor might not owe me an explanation, but I decided to have some fun with it. I contacted my acquaintance named Spud, who worked as a high-end street pharmacist, and obtained a few tablets of ketamine, just in case. I then went to the clinic at 5 o'clock in the evening when the sun was setting. Like a predator stalking its prey, I observed Dr. Patterson leaving the clinic and followed him from a short distance, making sure to keep a few cars between us. He eventually pulled into a housing track not far from the clinic, where my ex- girlfriend Liz lived, just four houses down across the street from Dr. Patterson's place. I knew the gate code and the neighborhood well. Patterson parked in his driveway, and I pulled up casually behind him, as if I were passing through the area.

"Hey, is that you, Dr. Patterson?" I yelled out, rolling down the passenger window. Patterson approached my car, slightly confused.

"Do I know you?" He asked, bending down to look inside.

"What? It's me, Tyrus Hemmingbird. I donated $300,000 to the clinic on Saturday," I replied, trying to jog his memory.

"Oh my, I'm sorry, I didn't recognize you at first. What are you doing here?" He inquired.

"Well, my girlfriend Liz lives just down the street on the opposite side," I explained. "Oh, Liz, I know her. Nice woman," Patterson replied.

"You know, Doc, I was actually on my way to her house, but do you mind if I have a word with you?" I asked.

"Sure, that's no problem. Come right in," he said, unlocking the door, and we walked up the stairs to his house.

"This is a nice place you've got here, Doc."

"Oh, thank you very much. Allow me to show you around," Dr. Patterson kindly offered as they entered the house.

Dr. Patterson looked around the spacious, 5000 ft. house. Walking in, they entered the beautiful open floor plan. To the left was Tyrus' study, equipped with a computer, books, and a small library. On the right was the elegant dining room.

Straight ahead lay the huge living room, while to the right of it was the well-furnished kitchen. Double doors led from the back of the nook into a large billiard room. Adjoining the billiard room was a door that led to a stunning guest bathroom and bedroom, with its own separate entrance. Adjacent to the dining room were two guest bedrooms, connected to a hallway leading to a three-car garage. On the left of the study, a hallway descended 10 feet, revealing the master suite, complete with a substantial walk-in closet, his and her sinks, and a luxurious Jacuzzi tub positioned perfectly in the middle of the bathroom.

"It's a very nice, modernized home, Tyrus. You know this house is only five years old, and I got an outstanding deal on it. By the way, do you happen to play pool?" Dr. Patterson asked curiously.

"Yeah, I do, but I'm not that good—at least I don't think I'm in your league," Tyrus modestly replied.

"Would you like something to drink?" Dr. Patterson offered.

"Sure, Doc, that would be fine," Tyrus accepted gratefully.

"I tell you what, I'm going to grab a couple of glasses of wine, and we can head back to the billiard room and shoot a few games of pool," Dr. Patterson suggested enthusiastically.

"Okay, let me just make a quick call to Liz and let her know I'll be there shortly. I'm right down the street," Tyrus said, taking out his phone and pretending to have a conversation with Liz, ensuring that it was loud enough for Patterson to overhear. When Dr. Patterson returned with the wine, Tyrus was already racking the balls.

"So, Mr. Hemmingbird, what is it that you would like to talk to me about?" Dr. Patterson inquired, taking a sip of his wine.

"I paid a visit to the clinic today, but neither you nor the director were there yet. I'm curious about your assessment of how the clinic is being run," Tyrus asked, calculating his words carefully, for his response could potentially determine Dr. Patterson's fate.

"The clinic could always use more help, but I don't see that happening anytime soon. The mayor is the one who calls the shots and pushes the buttons. All I do is follow their orders. My concern is not how things are done; as long as my check is ready, I'll continue to do what is told of me. That's just the way it is," Dr. Patterson candidly replied, breaking the balls and taking another sip of his wine.

"The nine-ball, in the side pocket," Dr. Patterson remarked, peering over his glasses and lining up the shot, successfully sinking the ball.

"Do you think it's possible, Doc, that I can have another glass of your fine wine?" Tyrus requested, with a hint of mischief in his voice.

"Sure, wow, you're quite thirsty!" Dr. Patterson replied, seemingly fascinated by Tyrus' sudden interest in more wine. Oblivious to Tyrus' actions, Dr. Patterson left to fetch another glass of wine.

As Dr. Patterson returned, wine in hand, Tyrus surreptitiously dropped the crushed-up ketamine into Patterson glass when he left the room. Dr. Patterson returned and offered Tyrus the freshly poured wine.

"Here you go. By the way, should I refer to you as Mr. Hemmingbird or just Tyrus?" Dr. Patterson asked, unaware of the secret ingredient in Tyrus' wine.

"Tyrus is fine. So, does anyone really care about the people at the clinic?" Tyrus questioned, trying to gauge Dr. Patterson's true feelings.

"A few of the nurses genuinely care and do their job well," Dr. Patterson responded.

"Now, I'm not particularly fond of a group of Pacific individuals who attempt to detach themselves from the three-dimensional paradigm we live in through unhealthy eating habits. But to each their own, right?" Tyrus commented, trying to keep the conversation flowing.

"Oh, my goodness, you finally missed," Tyrus remarked, noticing Dr. Patterson's shot go awry. "You mean to tell me I get a shot? So, do the mayor and the director share the same sentiments?"

Standing at the end of the table, Tyrus positioned himself to take his shot, holding the cue stick on his right side with the butt resting on the ground. As he glanced at Dr. Patterson, he observed the drug taking effect.

"I mean, do they know what's really happening at the clinic?" Tyrus pushed further, trying to gather more information.

"Yeah, pretty much. We had a meeting last week, and both the director and the mayor expressed their own strong feelings towards the African American community," Dr. Patterson admitted nonchalantly.

"What do you mean?" Tyrus questioned, feigning innocence.

"They simply don't care, and neither do I," Dr. Patterson proclaimed.

"The three-ball, in the corner, one bounce off the cushion. You're playing with me, right?" Tyrus rhetorically asked, making his move.

"Man, I don't feel so good," Dr. Patterson suddenly stated, hitting the floor, completely unaware of Tyrus' scheme.

Tyrus took all his clothes off, picked his body up, putting him in a big white cushion chair taking from the living room table. Duck tapping his arms and legs to the chair. He then walked out to his car, grabbing his bag of killing tools. Closing all the blinds, tying a rag through his mouth when Dr. Patterson awoke to try to speak. Tyrus looked at him holding his head.

"Two of my good friends told me how bad things were at the clinic, and I told them I would take care of it. So here I am taking care of it." Tyrus had just finished cleaning up everything he had touched with gloves on.

"Now, Doc, I'm going to take the rag out of your mouth if your screen or yell, I will cut your throat in the blink of an eye is that understood." The Doctor nodded his head, yes. The Doc was I was struggling to try to get loose from the chair. Tyrus took the rag out of his mouth.

"Stop your struggling Doc, you not getting a lose." "What the fuck are you doing, you crazy fuck."

"Now, that's not nice, Doc." Putting the rag back in his mouth Tyrus grabbed his razor-sharp Kukri knife putting it on his left leg, bringing it across to his other leg pushing down very Hard screaming with no sound coming out and shaking his head.

"No, no," Tyrus pulled the rag out of his mouth again.

"What, is it you are trying to say Doctor?" Pronouncing every syllable in the word doctor. Blood ran down his leg. Tyrus looked down at the blood, running down his leg. His eye turns bloodshot red. He Begins to speak with an old English accent.

"What the fuck are you, what's going on. I Didn't do anything to deserve this?"

"Says who, you know Doc I never took that shot, let me see if I can bank it off of the cushion." Speaking a strong English accent. He walked over to take the shot on the pool table. "Goddamit, I missed it."

Tyrus slowly cut him across his chest from his shoulder to the start of his top rib. He yells out.

"Please stop please, what the fuck did I do? What?"

"Now, I must admit I did go slow on that one," with a wicked smile on his face.

"You know what I love, Doc?" Cutting him very fast across the other shoulder and chest. "Your pain gives me pleasure."
Tyrus leans back against the pool table and looks at him. The doctor is in pain.

"You, sick motherfucker! Son of a bitch!"

"Oh, stop! It, Doc. Speaking calmly, no one is coming for you. And besides that, you know what. Sticks and stones may break my bones. But names will never hurt me." He laughs wickedly.

"Back in 1888, my best friend used to always say that to me. I'm just punishing you. Doing what it is that you do You know." Moving the knife around in a circle while he's talking to him.

"Killing for fun," with the weird, sinister, creepy Laugh. "See, you have a license to practice killing. I don't need a license to do what I do. I'm practicing too on how to kill people. In other words, we are both experimenting with people, like your guinea pigs, down at the clinic. But you don't look at it like that now, do you? You can experiment, but I can't. So, stop your fucking bickering."

Dr. Patterson tries to speak. Tyrus put his finger up to his mouth, shushing him. "No, no, no, don't do that doc. Did I tell you to speak? Now I've got to put the rag back in your mouth. This might sting a little."

He was walking behind him, carving BM on his back, screaming with no sound walking back around to the front of him, tapping the knife on the chair.

"Now, Doc., that wasn't so bad was it?" Sticking the blade down in his knee, very hard and looking at him in the face. Tyrus heard something.

"My goodness, doc. Someone is coming in the house through the front door. You didn't tell me you were expecting company." Creeping to his bag, grabbing two knives.

"Hello, where are you?" In a low voice.

When the gentlemen walked into the billet room, seeing all the blood and Dr. Patterson tied to a chair. He yelled out. "Oh my."

Before he could get God out of his mouth, Tyrus had through a knife straight dead center of his chest and a second knife 3 inches to the left of the first one before his body could hit the ground. He looked down at both knives in his chest.

"I love it; I love it, I love it." Laughing with the strong English accent.

"Who was that doctor? Don't tell me," Laughing very loud and limping walking over to the body on the floor, pulling both knives out of his chest.

"Now, let's see, where were we?" Holding his chin up. Which eye did you want to lose first? The left or the right. He was pulling the blade out of his knee, putting it as close as he could to his left eye.

"No, Dr., I'm not going to do that." Turning his back to him, with his knife in his right hand. Gripping it tightly,

"Tyrus is no longer heard. It's me, his great, great grandfather Fred." He turns and swings, with everything he has. Leaving his Head hanging by just the bone that his knife didn't cut through. Standing over the doctor, watching the blood run down his body.

"I'm the real boogie man." He takes a deep breath. He is stripping down naked, grabbing a plastic bag and putting all his clothes in the bag. He goes and takes a shower. Making sure not to leave any of his DNA anywhere at the scene, taking the soapy washcloth, and pouring bleach down the drain. Changing his clothing as if nothing has ever happened. He is limping back, taking one last look and leaving the billiard room, a bloodied mess.

He walks to the doorway of the billiard room, looking back, saying to himself now that's a bloodied mess for the ages. They're going to have fun cleaning that up. Tyrus snaps out of it.

"What the hell happened?" He says out loud.

Looking at the doctor, all cut up, Tyrus grabbing his bag in a panic, leaving the doctor's house. With no clue about what just happened. Tyrus had started to feel the rush of the addiction for killing. He thought to himself if I knew where the director was, I would go and find him tonight right this minute. But Friday is good. I'll make that his last day. Nodding his head tapping on the Sternwheel to a Roberta Flack song playing on the car stereo, killing me softly. Headed back to the mansion. The help had gone for the rest of the night. Tyrus headed upstairs, changing into a white V-neck T-shirt and black pajama bottoms, Tyrus made his way to the kitchen where he prepared a cup of sleepy time tea. With his tea in hand, he descended downstairs to his secret room. Sitting at the desk, he perused old photos of his great, great grandfathers' victims while taking sips of his tea.

After some time, Tyrus stood up and pressed the button at the top of the staircase, closing the door to the room. Feeling a wave of tiredness, he lay down on the bed. As he drifted off to sleep, he entered a vivid and unsettling dream. In the dream, he found himself being choked by a rope from behind. In a desperate attempt to free himself, he fought back, but his efforts seemed futile. The fear intensified as he struggled for breath and attempted to call for help, yet his voice failed him. Finally, he jolted awake, heart racing, his body covered in sweat, relieved that it had only been a dream.

Shaken by the experience, Tyrus couldn't shake the feeling that someone was watching him even after waking up. Despite the empty space behind him, he couldn't shake the paranoia.

Unable to get much sleep that Thursday night, Tyrus

decided to rise early at 4:30 AM on Friday. He was determined to reach the mansion before James, wanting to retrieve some items for his next plan, concerning his next victim, Todd Foster. As Tyrus descended into the secret room, memories and doubts about Foster stirred within him. He recalled encountering Foster before and the uneasy feeling he had about him.

Deciding to do some research, Tyrus turned to his computer. As he delved into it, he discovered previous charges against Foster for embezzlement and his involvement in a child pornography ring. The more Tyrus read, the more disgusted and determined he became. He knew he wanted to end Foster's life swiftly, recognizing the injustice that the mayor, Ed Williams, had allowed such a despicable person to flourish under his watch.

With his mind made up, Tyrus made it to the mansion in time before James arrived. He proceeded down to the secret room, but as he glanced at the bed, thoughts of his recent nightmare took hold. Suddenly, his eyes caught sight of a blood message on the wall next to the bed, reading, "You don't deserve that body you're walking around in." Panic and confusion washed over Tyrus as he frantically searched for answers.

Terrified, he hurriedly left the room, stumbling on the last step as he emerged from the secret space. Distressed and on edge, Tyrus noticed James entering through the front door.

"Good morning, Sir," greeted James concernedly. "I heard you yelling. Is everything okay?"

Trying to compose himself, Tyrus replied, "Yes, everything's fine." However, the weariness and stress on his face were apparent.

James sensed something was off, jokingly asking, "You sure everything's alright? You look a bit tired. Were you out partying last night?"

Tyrus sighed, feeling worn out. "No, just didn't get much rest last night, that's all. Has anyone broken in or caused any trouble?"

Thankfully, James assured him, "No, sir, everything is fine. I just arrived. I had to drop off my granddaughter at school this morning. She's growing up so fast."

Relieved by the normalcy of the situation, Tyrus gathered his thoughts. He had plans to pay a visit to Mr. Foster while dressed in his distinctive outfit. It would provide him with a sense of satisfaction. However, the image of the blood message on the wall and the constant feeling of being watched continued to haunt him.

The day passed as Tyrus prepared for what would be his second kill in a week. He knew exactly when the clinic would close, giving him an opportunity to arrange a meeting with Foster. Tyrus called Foster to set up a late appointment, disguising it as a meeting to discuss a donation to the clinic. Foster, impressed by Tyrus's speech at the mayor's dinner, agreed to meet him at 7:00 PM.

Mark and I arrived at the clinic at 5:30 PM to visit Mark's uncle, Frank. The two of them were engaged in a friendly game of dominoes. Throughout our visit, I took plenty of photos capturing the precious moments shared between

Mark and his uncle. We were at the clinic for four and a half hours. The clinic itself resembled a single-story hospital, with two patients occupying each room, separated by curtains. As we entered through the double doors, the lobby welcomed us, while the waiting room, equipped with 20 chairs, was situated to the left. In the top left corner of the waiting room, a television was mounted. Adjacent to the waiting room, there stood a security stand where a guard kept watch. The rooms numbered from one to twenty were located on the left side, while rooms twenty-one to forty were positioned on the right. The layout of the clinic formed a circular arrangement. The offices were situated at the back, accessible from the section where one originally entered, but only between the hours of 9 AM and 5 PM. Outside of these hours, one had to navigate through the lobby.

When Tyrus arrived, the guys in the clinic stared at him as he walked past security. Fortunately for Tyrus, there were no security cameras monitoring the premises.

Mark's uncle, Frank, was in room 18. As Tyrus made his way to the offices, the director's office was positioned down a long hallway across from the utility closet. Tyrus approached the big solid wood door with no window and knocked. Foster, the director, responded, "Please come in."

Upon entering the office, Tyrus couldn't help but notice the splendid decorations. Fake awards adorned the right wall as soon as one walked through the door, and Mr. Foster's computer sat on the right side of his desk. The nameplate, reading "Director Foster," was positioned in the middle of the desk. Six silver balls on Mr. Foster's desk clicked together as they swung back and forth, providing a touch of kinetic energy. To the left of the desk, there was a stylish wooden receipt spike.

"Hello, Mr. Foster," Tyrus greeted in a soft voice. "My employer wanted me to drop off a check."

"Oh, okay. I thought he would be here," Mr. Foster replied.

"How are you this evening?" Tyrus inquired, trying to establish a friendly rapport. He moved towards the left side of Mr. Foster's desk, attempting to make himself more comfortable.

"Are you one of those gentlemen who keeps a nice bottle of cognac, or some other liquor hidden in your bottom left drawer?" Tyrus took a playful chance, hoping for a positive response.

"You know what? You're absolutely right," Mr. Foster replied with a smile. "Let's get it started."

Tyrus has managed to ease, all the way up on Mr. Foster. He is standing in striking distance. Foster reaches down to the bottom drawer to grab the liquor. Tyrus grabs him by the back of his head, ramming the receipt spike through his left eye. He screams out, Tyrus covers his mouth, cutting his throat. He slumps over dead at his desk, with blood running all over the place. Tyrus takes a deep breath, standing behind his body. He closes his eyes then slowly, opening them stabbing him in the back of his neck, as his blade goes cleared through his throat. Starting from his collar, Tyrus grabs the scissors off the desk. Cutting his shirt, straight down his back while the body leaned over, carving BM in his back. He then cut a patch of his hair, putting it in a plastic bag, and cleaning off the scissors. Looking at his work of art, he chuckles.

"You knew I was a man!" Smiling, "You sick fuck. But then

again, you probably didn't because I look sexy and good. You probably even thought you were going to get some pussy, did you?" Laughing Hysterically. "No, not this hot stuff," pointing his knife at him.

"You probably thought I was going to be easy. I didn't, tell you I don't fuck on the first date!"

Laughing with an active evil English accent. Now walking with a limp. He puts his knife back under his red dress. He then straightens up his blonde wig, with his red lipstick on and diamond earrings leaving a sweet scent lingering behind. He looks down at his red heels that have blood on them. Walks back to Mr. Foster's desk, grabbing a Kleenex. Wiping off his heels. Locking the door from the inside. Walking down the hallway, currently, he walks right past Mark and me. Who was standing in the hall, talking to Tori that attended our school? My camera started taking photos and videos. The camera just started taking pictures. Tyrus looked back at me and smiled. To see if he had taken a picture of him. But my camera was pointing down. So, he kept walking. Right out the back door, where his car was parked. I looked at Tori and says to her, "You know, sometimes I think this camera is possessed; it has a mind of its own."

"Now, Marcus, you have been taking photos of everyone since you've got this camera. But you haven't taken any of me yet."

"You know Tori, you're right. I apologize, let's go back around by the offices and take some shots, Mark, we will be right back."

We walked towards the offices we stopped and took photos

in front of the artwork on the wall; two chairs are sitting outside of Foster's office.

"Hey Tori, let's see how creative you could be. Let's take some photos of you sitting in these chairs."

After taking eight shots. "Now I'm going to do a video; you can say your name. And then tell everyone what your plans are after high school."

"What about this?"

She is sitting in one chair turning right, putting both of her legs over the arms. And her feet in the other chair.

"You think that's okay, or is that corny?"

"No, that good. I'm ready."

When I turn the camera on and start recording. Tori began to talk to the camera. I could see the hole murder scene from the beginning to the end. How it happened and everything like that. Had happened, I heard nothing that Tori said. Standing there looking, "Tori I'm sorry, shaking we got to go, we got to get out here fast."

"Why what's wrong? Marcus."

"I'll explain to you later." I ran around to Mark's uncles' room. "Mark, I need to talk to you for a minute."

"What's up chief?" Smiling, walking up to me, giving me a handshake.

Tori is standing there; Mark and I begin the conversation. I grabbed Mark by the arm, pulling him to the side. Whispering, "Man, I just saw another murder here in the clinic."

I was looking around frightened. Mark puts both of his hands together, wiping coming down over the face and pushing me in the chess. I'm standing there looking at him.

"Man, please don't start this mess! Let me look at it, Marcus?"

"Come on, man, you know you can't see it."

"You can bet that because nothing is there. Let me see." I show Mark the video. "Tori, come look at this. And tell me what you see."

Tori walks over, standing in between Mark and me.

"What are you guys talking about? Hello Marcus. Let me see? Well, I see a beautiful black sister that is looking way too good smiling and laughing."

"And that's what I see. You can bet that," looking at me with a look of I told you so. "Okay, Man." Putting both of his hands in the air. "I'm out."

Three hours later, as the cleaning lady came by cleaning up the offices. Mark was still visiting his uncle at the clinic. It was 10:30 PM, the clinic was quiet. Suddenly, there was a scream. People that were there visiting their loved ones started coming out of the rooms. What's going on, as a security guard came running down the hallway. The clean lady stood there in the doorway, screaming. Everyone came out, asking questions.

"What's going on? What's happened?" The cleaning lady uncontrollable shaking. Somebody calls the police. A security guard covers her eyes, holding her tight walking her, away from the door. Mark walked down, looking around, wanting to investigate the room. "What happened? Does anybody know what happened?" Looking noisily, walking looking in the place himself. He throws up from the site of all the blood.

"Oh my God, what the fuck?" He runs away from the door, taking his cell phone out of his pocket, calling me.

"Man, pick up Marcus pick up." But I did not answer. Mark Crying with tears coming down his face. He goes back into his uncles' room.

"Man!" Shaking scared as hell, "Someone killed somebody in the office rooms. I got to go. I'll call you later!"

 Mind Game

James was assigned the daunting task by Tyrus's sister, Victoria, to meticulously cleanse the bloodstains from the wall. The unyielding mental strain Tyrus experienced only reaffirmed Victoria's success in making him believe that he was losing his mind. What Tyrus was unaware of was that Victoria had long known about the elusive secret room, as she had discovered it five years prior. When James stumbled upon it during the cleaning process, Victoria instructed him to leave the sacred space untouched, just as their great-great-grandfather had.

In a twist of fate, James, being privy to the intricate web of financial control, dutifully followed Victoria's orders. She had subtly planted clues about the secret room for years, hoping that Tyrus would eventually stumble upon it, but he never did. That's when Victoria took matters into her own hands. Through extensive study of brain activity and the inner workings of the mind, she developed an invention she called the "Brainstem"—a machine capable of manipulating thoughts and ideas.

Taking her research further, Victoria implanted a minuscule chip, smaller than a grain of rice, into a soft spot behind Tyrus's left ear. With this chip, imperceptible from the outside, Victoria had the power to influence and shape Tyrus's thoughts, bringing them forward to the surface of his consciousness. She could whisper thoughts and ideas into his mind, molding his reality and influencing his actions. Beyond that, she even crafted a mechanism within the chip to make him believe he was hearing voices, further deepening her control over him.

Victoria meticulously documented her experiments and research on Tyrus in a 300-page file stored safely within her research lab. Whenever Tyrus visited, James would discreetly drug him with a cappuccino, causing him to fall into a deep sleep without any recollection of missing time. It was during these moments of vulnerability that Victoria performed necessary procedures to further implant her manipulative suggestions into Tyrus's subconscious mind, ensuring her complete control over his thoughts and actions.

The secret room, a core element in Victoria's grand plan, was under constant surveillance through strategically placed video cameras. Hours were spent by Victoria trying to locate a hidden compartment within the room, to no avail. Thus, when Tyrus stumbled upon the secret passage door while in the room, Victoria carefully observed his every movement, excited by the breakthrough and inching closer to her ultimate goal.

Victoria had deemed Tyrus unworthy of the Hemmingbird legacy due to his lack of ambition and excessive indulgence. Her solution? To mold him into the family's designated killer, akin to his infamous great-great-grandfather, Fred Hemmingbird. Each puzzle piece had meticulously been put in place, with Victoria even introducing a STEM scholarship program to find potential recruits who she could further manipulate and ensnare in her web of control. By establishing the program, she sought out bright young minds in science, technology, engineering, and math—perfect candidates to serve her hidden ulterior motives. Coincidentally, I happened to be one of the top three students selected for the prestigious Hemmingbird STEM scholarship

After the director's unfortunate passing, Tyrus was driving home when he made a stop to refuel his car. It was then that he noticed a homeless lady pushing a shopping cart, containing a 5-gallon water bottle filled with change predominantly consisting of nickels and pennies. Intrigued, Tyrus initiated a conversation with her.

"Excuse me, how much change do you think you have there?" He inquired.

The homeless lady shrugged, "I don't know."

"If you had to guess, would you say it's maybe $400 or $500?" Tyrus ventured.

"Really? Okay, I don't think it's that much," Tyrus stated honestly.

"I didn't ask you what you think," the homeless lady retorted sharply.

Realizing his misstep, Tyrus quickly apologized.

"You're right, I'm sorry. I'm on your side. How about I give you $1000 right now for that change?"

Her initial suspicion melted into a smile, as she gently hit her right hand across her leg in appreciation. "Don't play with me like that, I'll cut you right where you stand," she warned, albeit more lightheartedly.

Amused by her candidness, Tyrus fetched $1000 from his red purse and handed it to her. The homeless lady gratefully accepted the generous gesture, and Tyrus proceeded to load the jug of money into his car. Just before departing, she pointed out Tyrus' attire, prompting him to chuckle and play along.

"Girl, I've got to look the part to get my money somehow," he quipped back.

"Well, those heels look like they're killing your feet; you should take them off when you get home," she advised earnestly.

Agreeing with a smile, Tyrus bid her farewell and drove off, eventually reaching his abode to change out of his outfit. He then pampered himself by soaking his feet in the jacuzzi, reflecting on the discomfort of walking in heels all night. As he pondered his next move—a plan to eliminate the mayor—the unexpected arrival of Victoria interrupted his thoughts.

Engaging in casual banter, Victoria mentioned her plans for the top three STEM scholarship winners and extended an invitation for Tyrus to assist her. Despite his reservations, she eventually persuaded him to consider the opportunity, promising an enjoyable experience and a chance to mingle with future talents.

After drying off and joining Victoria at the mansion's bar, the news bulletin revealing the tragic demise of director Todd Foster captured their attention. The chilling details of the murder, attributed to an unknown assailant leaving the initials BM at the crime scene, left them unsettled. As the mayor's reaction was broadcast, Tyrus felt a surge of disdain towards him, intensifying his resolve to take decisive action while maintaining caution.

Secluded on his porch, I mulled over the implications of the murder and hesitated to inform My parents, pondering the missed calls from Mark and my mom that popped up on his phone. The weight of recent events lingered in the air as I contemplated his next steps with a mix of determination and apprehension. After witnessing the deathly scene captured by the office room's cameras, I hesitated to share the information with my parents. Instead, I chose to sit on the porch outside, mulling over the interconnectedness of the murders, which seemed to fit together like pieces of a cryptic puzzle.

I divulged the news of my selection for the Hemmingbird scholarship to Mark, who expressed concern about the path I was treading. Nevertheless, I tried lightening the mood, joking about potentially gaining insider information if I attended the dinner. Mark's apprehension persisted, yet he congratulated me on the honor. We finished our conversation with the intricate handshake we had developed, reassured that our friendship extended beyond the realm of secrets and danger.

Resolute and determined, I stepped inside my house, ready to engage in a conversation with my mother that would undoubtedly alter the course of my life.

A week had passed before Dr. Patterson's body was discovered, and security around the mayor had significantly increased. Tyrus knew that in order to execute his plan and reach the mayor, he needed him to be alone without any disturbance. So, Tyrus began closely observing the mayor's regular routines, determined to identify the perfect opportunity. Throughout that week, Tyrus diligently watched the mayor, gathering valuable information about his habits and even discovering that his wife would be undergoing surgery at the hospital. Media coverage provided Tyrus with such details, as they tended to keep the public well-informed about those in power. Upon learning about the surgery, Tyrus realized this would be one of the few instances when the mayor would be alone and vulnerable. His mind started concocting a strategy.

Every morning, there was always at least one security officer sitting in a car near the mayor's residence, ensuring his safety during the early hours. However, late at night, after 10:30 P.M., security dwindled, leaving just one person in the car stationed in front of the house. The mayor's mansion, standing tall for over a century, held historical significance not only for the city but also for Tyrus's family. He couldn't help but recall stories passed down through generations about his great-great-grandfather's time as the mayor. The Hemmingbird family had diligently kept a record of significant events that occurred within their lineage. This connection ignited a sense of determination within Tyrus as he delved into old records, uncovering fascinating details about how the mansion had been structured in the past. To his amazement, he stumbled upon information about an old tunnel that ran underneath the mayor's residence. A sigh of excitement escaped his lips; this could be his pathway inside, he thought, devising a plan in his mind.

Wrigley's house, as everyone called it, was a magnificent structure built in 1896. It consisted of three stories, a basement, ten bedrooms, and fifteen bathrooms, sprawled over an impressive 15,000 square feet. Its entrance boasted a grand marble foyer, leading visitors into a splendid cherry oak staircase that gracefully ascended to the second floor. The first floor held a beautiful carom billiard table, serving as the focal point of the billiard room adorned with artwork featuring former mayors. Hardwood floors adorned the entire mansion, evoking a sense of timeless elegance. Determined to carry out his plan, Tyrus parked his car discreetly in close proximity to the estate. He meticulously disguised himself as a homeless person, even wearing his great-great-grandfather's old trench coat as a shroud of anonymity. With cautious steps, he made his way towards the old tunnel located in the Chicago metropolitan area, ensuring he had a pair of latex gloves for added precautions.

Entering the tunnel, Tyrus gradually immersed himself in the darkness. Illuminated only by the faint glow of his flashlight, he ventured deeper, gaining confidence with every step. Suddenly, he encountered a gate obstructing his path, secured by a rusty lock and an entwined chain. Determined not to let this barrier impede his progress, he struck the lock with his Gurkha kukri knife, breaking it effortlessly. Now unhindered, he continued his trek through the tunnel, cautious with each movement, like a silent cat prowling through the night. As he journeyed further, he stumbled upon a door marked with iron bars and another lock. Undeterred, Tyrus skillfully picked the lock, orchestrating a delicate dance between the lock and the lock pick until the door swung open with a whisper. Ensuring his presence remained undetected, he tiptoed into the room he discovered, largely untouched and forgotten for years. It was a hidden haven, shrouded in silence. Deep inside the mansion, Tyrus stood surrounded by a haunting stillness, his flashlight providing the only source of illumination. The room had been blocked off during renovations long ago, a relic of the mansion's history.

To his surprise, he realized there was a faint glow emitting from a slit in the wall that separated the room from an adjacent space. As he peered through the opening, voices traveling through the airwaves reached his ears. A burst of realization struck him - he had unknowingly infiltrated the confines of the mayor's mansion. The room to which he had gained access had been sealed off during renovations, undoubtedly for security purposes. Silently, he listened, eavesdropping on the conversation emanating from the other side of the wall. The mayor's voice resonated with authority and confidence, compelling Tyrus to inch closer towards the source of the discussion. Restraining his excitement, he avoided making any sound that could potentially expose his presence or compromise his intentions. Gradually, through the narrow gap, he caught a glimpse of the mayor conversing with his security details, explaining their respective assignments for the night. The mayor informed his head security, Michael McNeil, that he would spend the remainder of the night inside the mansion and requested him to conduct a final perimeter check before securing the premises. The mayor expressed gratitude for Michael's unwavering commitment before bidding him goodnight.

Immersed in the unfolding events, Tyrus watched attentively as the mayor's security personnel departed through the front door of the mansion. A sense of anticipation washed over him. In the subsequent silence, he could hear the mayor's footsteps resonating through the hallways as he ascended the grand staircase. One by one, the lights downstairs flickered off, plunging the mansion into darkness. Acknowledging the opportune moment, Tyrus cautiously retraced his steps, heading back towards his car, momentarily leaving the vicinity. Once there, he retrieved his bag and the jar of coins he had obtained from the homeless lady, mentally preparing himself for the next phase of his plan. Taking measured steps, he reentered the mansion, ensuring each movement remained inconspicuous. Upstairs, he could still hear the echoing melodies of the mayor's shower serenade, his distinctive rendition of

"The Devil Went Down to Georgia."

Taking off his shoes, Tyrus silently ascended the grand staircase, his heart pounding with anticipation.

Arriving on the landing, he discreetly peeked through the narrow slit, gaining a glimpse of the mayor's bedroom. There, he witnessed a private moment as the mayor dropped his towel and discarded his robe before stepping into the shower. Remaining just outside the bathroom door, standing within the ample space of the master bedroom, Tyrus carefully surveyed his surroundings. The king-size bed commanded attention against the far wall, exuding an aura of regality, while a cozy sofa adorned the left side of the bed, accompanied by a small end table topped with a lamp. Positioned in front of the couch was a long coffee table, its surface embellished with a brass tree that held delicate name tags hanging from each branch. On the right side of the room, Tyrus patiently awaited the mayor's emergence from the shower, biding his time until the moment of execution.

As the Mayor stepped out of the shower, still singing and toothbrush in hand, Tyrus quietly revealed himself, emerging from his well-practiced hiding position. Silently and swiftly, he closed the distance, poised to fulfill the intentions that had fueled him thus far. With the knife to the mayor's throat very hard. "Don't move if you blink wrong; I will cut your fucking throat right where you stand."

"Please, please don't kill me."

"Shut up, you are fucking coward; don't you look at me. You're a piece of shit. Sit your ass down on the end of that bed."

Tyrus knocked him in the head very hard, knocking him out and stuffing a handkerchief in his mouth, putting tape over his mouth. The mayor wakes up, trying to stop him.

"Move your god damn hands down!"

The mayor then recognizes that it's Tyrus, moving his head trying to talk. Tyrus punches him across his temple knocking him out again, down on the bed. He ties the mayor's hands and feet up to the bed. Tyrus then goes back downstairs to where Tyrus entered the mansion, grabbing the jug full of coins and taking it back upstairs, where Tyrus has the mayor. He walks over to the mayor, who is still unconscious. Tyrus's open palm slaps him hard, waking him up. The mayor was scared and frightened for his life, his eyes wide open. Tyrus is standing next to the bed, looking down over him and snatching the tape off his mouth and pulling off some of the hair on his face.

"What the fuck is this about, Tyrus? What are you doing?"

"Didn't I tell you to shut the hell up! Speak when you are spoken to, Mayor." Tyrus closes his eyes, taking a deep breath as if he were meditating or something, he pulls his knife out. He is moving the back of the blade across the mayor's chest.

"Mark 8:36," he says what good is it for a man to gain the whole world yet forfeit his soul? Mr. Mayor. See, understand this; you are around here taking money that doesn't belong to you. Money that you don't even need, and you're doing it for greed, and that's bad. Do you know who I am, Mr. Mayor?"

"Yes, I do, Tyrus," sarcastically, he says.

"You took my family $300,000 like it was nothing, and on top of that, the whole clinic is a fraud just a front I don't like that, and it upsets me. Oh, you don't know I've wanted to get to you when I found out your fraudulent activities!" Speaking very low and calm. See you don't know who I am? Well, let me tell you. I'm the boogie man that everyone fears."

The mayor has a stubborn look on his face.

"I don't give a fuck who you are."

"Oh, I like that." Cutting the mayor across his chest down to rib cage. The site blood makes Tyrus voice change, to a broad English accent. He is now walking with a limp. Tyrus stands over him, squinting his eyes and looking down at the mayor.

"I remember you, Ed." In a deep voice.

"I remember when I used to take my knuckle and putting it on your head, giving you the screwdriver grinding my knuckle on your head. You were just a young whippersnapper; you don't remember me. Well, of course, I look a little different now! With an evil voice. We used to tease you all the time, Ed, Ed, who wet the bed."

The mayor's eyes lit up Bright as headlights.

"Now, terrified. No This can't be." Mayor Yelled out. "How could this be!"

"I'm the boogie man Ed, and I'm going to make this painful as possible!" Laughing hysterically, sinisterly insane.

Tyrus was looking up at the ceiling, speaking in a calm, pleasant voice. Tyrus Rolling his head around in a circular motion as if it was on a swivel.

"Now, Ed, I have to cover your mouth I wouldn't want you to yell out."

He is laughing, soft, and low. Putting two fingers over his mouth and shushing himself and looking into the mayor's eyes. Death comes quickly. He is standing up on the bed over the mayor's body, taking his razor-sharp knife stabbing him in his throat, pulling the blade all the way down to his penis, and filleting him open like a sardine and ripping open his rib cage. Taking a deep breath, looking up at the ceiling.

"I love it; I love it. I love it!"

He steps off to bed, walking over grabbing the jug field with coins, pouring the coins inside of the mayor's body, and taking 2 $100 bills stuffing them inside of his mouth.

"Now Mr. Mayor, that's what stealing money gets you. And that greed for your ass. Deadman!"

He takes his knife carving BM on the mayor's left thigh. He leaves the mayor's resident unnoticed.

I Never Knew

My mom rented a black tuxedo with a white shirt for me to wear to the big dinner. I was feeling nervous, so I decided to go to bed early on Friday night in an attempt to focus my positive energy. However, the image of Fred in my camera and the recent murder at the hospital were still fresh in my mind. As I lay in bed, looking up at the ceiling, my body remained still, but my mind was racing at a hundred miles an hour, trying to make sense of all the unexplained events.

By the time sleep finally fell upon my eyelids, it was midnight, and I found myself back in the old recurring dream. In the dream, a lady was holding onto the clock hand, petrified and looking down at the ground. The clock read 9:15, and a man was standing under it, urging her to let go. But she looked at me and pleaded for help, calling me by name. As I walked closer towards the man, I caught a glimpse of his face in the glass door below the clock. It was Fred Hemmingbird, the same person I had seen in my camera. He seemed unaware of my presence until he turned and spotted me.

In the dream, Fred started chasing me, swinging his blade and growling with a sinister laugh. Everything seemed to move in slow motion, and I could feel the sweat on my body as I jumped up, sitting on the edge of my bed. My mom knocked on my door and entered the room, concerned about my well-being.

"Are you okay, Marcus?" She asked.

"I'm okay, just had a bad dream, that's all," I reassured her.

"Okay, try to get some sleep. You have a big day tomorrow."

I tried my best to go back to sleep, but I had no success. The next morning came fast, and as I walked downstairs, the smell of breakfast my dad was cooking filled the air. Upon seeing me, my dad remarked,

"Son, you look like you had a long rough night."

"No, just nervous about today, that's all," I replied, trying to keep the bad dreams and the murders I had seen to myself. No one else could see them, and no one else believed me. Except for one time when my mom thought we were in the twilight zone, as they showed what I had seen on the news. But apart from that, no one believed anything I said. Yet somehow, I felt like the camera was trying to tell me a story, perhaps something I hadn't put together yet. I walked over to the stove, fixed myself a plate, and took a seat at the kitchen table. Just then, my mom came downstairs, entering the kitchen. The oven was set to the right in the kitchen island, with four barstools lined up along the left side. To the left of that was the kitchen table. The refrigerator stood next to the stove, and the kitchen window curtains were drawn open, allowing the beautiful sunshine to illuminate the room. My dad greeted my mom with a kiss.

"Honey, they found the mayor murdered; it's been all over the news," my dad informed my mom.

"What? That's terrible," she replied in shock.

Turning her attention to me, she asked, "So, what's the number one thing you're looking forward to after you win the scholarship, Marcus?"

"Mom, I don't even know if I'm going to win it," I responded uncertainly.

"Marcus, baby, you've already won it," my mom reassured me, her eyes filled with pride.

"That's right, son. Believe in yourself," my dad chimed in, giving me a supportive nod.

"Okay, thanks, mom, dad," I said, feeling slightly more encouraged.

As I finished my breakfast, Mark, my friend, appeared walking up the block. My Dad jokingly remarked, "Son, here comes your friend blinking 1000 times a minute."

"Oh, honey, that's not nice, stop," my mom scolded playfully.

Mark knocked on the door and my dad invited him in. Mark walked straight into the kitchen and exclaimed, "Boy, do you have a smell detector at your house that tells you when we're cooking?"

"No, sir, but it does smell good and looks good too," Mark replied with his characteristic fast blinking.

"Good morning, everyone! Looks like I'm right on time," Mark said, smiling at Mr. Davis, who shook his head in amusement.

"Scooch over, son, I'll fix you a plate. You're something else, one of a kind," my dad said to Mark, as he took a seat at the table, raising his eyebrows in response.

"So, you ready, man?" Mark asked me.

"I'm just going to dinner," I answered, trying to downplay the significance of the occasion.

"Man, this is huge! Make sure you take lots of pictures," Mark responded enthusiastically.

Looking back at Mr. Davis, he added, "Mr. Davis, you sure are a good cook."

"Boy, do you ever stop blinking?" Mr. Davis jokingly asked Mark.

"Yeah, as a matter of fact, I do when I'm sleeping. You can bet that," Mark replied, making everyone laugh.

Meanwhile, I was reading about the mayor's death in the newspaper while sitting at the table. After the tragic incident, every law enforcement agency in Chicago was searching for BM, a mysterious figure who had left his mark on the city. No one had any clue about his true identity, with only the police linking the initials to the name Boogieman. The rest of the day seemed to fly by, and before I knew it, my family and I were stepping out of the car at the restaurant.

As we approached the door, my mom, dressed in a beautiful turquoise evening dress, gracefully moved with the wind. Clutching her turquoise and black clutch under her arm, she walked tall in her black heels. My dad, donning a black tuxedo, stood beside me while I carried my camera across my shoulder. Mr. Davis chivalrously opened the door for his wife and me. Together, we entered the restaurant, where Victoria Hemmingbird had reserved the entire venue for the night's event. Only the three families of the scholarship nominees would be present for the dinner.

The restaurant was a stunning, award-winning establishment called Kinzie, renowned for its exquisite selection of fine wines. White tablecloths adorned the tables, with black napkins placed elegantly beside each set of silverware. The wine glasses sparkled, catching the light from the unique, one-of-a-kind chandelier that hung overhead, creating a cozy and breathtaking ambiance.

As we walked through the downstairs area, we made our way to the upstairs dining room. A young lady in a light blue evening dress greeted us with the most beautiful smile as we entered.

"Good evening, my name is Victoria, and I will be your host for the evening," she introduced herself with a hand placed delicately across her chest. Beside her stood her brother Tyrus, who had his hands resting on her shoulders. Tyrus, dressed in a black tuxedo, bowed his head and greeted us, saying,

"It's good to meet everyone." Victoria then directed her attention to me, saying, "Now, this handsome young man must be Marcus."

"Yes," I replied, extending my hand to shake hers. She responded by grasping my hand with both of hers, saying, "It is a pleasure to meet you, Marcus." She then turned to my parents, inquiring, "And who do we have here?"

"This is my mom, Sandra," I said, introducing my mom, "and this is my dad, Paul."

"It is great to meet you both; I loved your son's essay," Victoria said, shaking Sandra's and Paul's hands. "It's so good to meet both of you," she added with a warm smile.

Introducing Tyrus once again, as he seemed a bit shy, Victoria continued with hospitality and grace.

"This is Tyrus, Mr. and Mrs. Davis," greeted Tyrus as my camera began snapping pictures. Sometimes my camera goes off for no apparent reason, almost as if it has a mind of its own. We were the first family to arrive at the elegant venue, where a long table awaited the gathering of families. The atmosphere felt like a scene from a movie, with everything perfectly arranged. It was the most impressive restaurant I had ever seen, with soft Jazz playing in the background and candles gently illuminating the table. It seemed like everyone spoke in hushed whispers, creating an aura of enchantment.

To the far left of the room, four booth tables provided a breathtaking view of the city through the windows. We chose to sit in the middle of the long table that extended through the room, while Victoria engaged in pleasant conversation with a newly arrived family.

"Mum, dad, this place looks expensive," I remarked, feeling a mix of excitement and curiosity.

"Yes, it does, dear. Just be yourself, and everything will fall into place," my parents assured me.

As I absorbed the surroundings and ambiance, I couldn't help but marvel at the exquisite layout of the restaurant. Our last name was elegantly displayed on the table, reserved just for us. The gleam in my eyes resembled that of watching a rocket launching towards the moon. It was an exhilarating experience. I gently tapped my mother on the shoulder and whispered, "That's Henry's mom, you remember them."

Waving at Henry's family, I followed Tyrus as he guided us to our table. Meanwhile, another family made their entrance, and Victoria warmly welcomed them. The waiter, named Byron, poured water for us as he introduced himself. Henry Gray and his family took their seats directly across from us. I had met Henry before at a science fair, and the prospect of seeing him again filled me with excitement. I couldn't resist the urge and sneaked around to strike up a conversation with him while waiting for the last family to arrive. The Davis and Gray families engaged in friendly small talk, triggering my camera to keep capturing unexpected photos. Eventually, I returned to the table to grab my camera.

"Mum, could you please take a picture of Henry and me?" I requested eagerly.

"Of course, Marcus. I'd be happy to," my mom replied with a loving smile.

"Thanks, Mom. I really appreciate it," I expressed my gratitude.

"Oh, Marcus, you're too sweet," she responded tenderly.

In the midst of our conversation, the Rongomas family entered the room and took their seats. Victoria, as the host, stood up to welcome everyone, while the waiters circulated, serving drinks and taking orders. She expressed her gratitude for everyone attending the Scholarship Dinner, where the winner would be granted a full-ride scholarship and apprenticeship to the prestigious Brain STEM research program. The second and third runners-up would also receive substantial monetary prizes. Victoria encouraged us all to enjoy the evening, promising to reveal the winner at the end of the dinner.

With everyone engaged in lively conversations, the room was filled with a festive buzz. The delightful wild mushroom & gorgonzola cheese tart appetizer tantalized our taste buds. My mom selected the smoked salmon Rigatona while my dad opted for the 18oz. Bone-in Delmonico steak. The menu offered an array of mouthwatering options, making it difficult for me to decide. Eventually, I settled on Kinzie's roasted chicken breast, which turned out to be the most delectable chicken breast I had ever tasted. Unable to contain my excitement, I snapped a photo of the exquisite food and sent it to Mark, who jokingly requested I save him a piece. We both shared a laugh, envisioning his startled reaction.

An hour and a half flew by as everyone savored their meals, and finally, desserts were served. Victoria stood up, capturing everyone's attention.

"Before I announce the winner of the Hemmingbird STEM program," she began, her voice projecting with confidence, "I'd like to express my sincerest gratitude to each and every one of you for joining us tonight."

Victoria stepped toward the podium situated on the left side of the room, taking a deep breath to gather her thoughts.

"Without further ado, it is my pleasure to announce the third runner-up for the STEM program, who will receive a $5000 check towards their college education, Nala Rongomas."

The room erupted in applause as Nala gracefully made her way to the podium. Nala, an African student who had recently moved from Kenya to our city, stood at 5'7" with a slender frame. Her hair was braided straight back, and she wore a stunning dark brown summer dress. The half-inch black heels she wore added a touch of elegance, while diamonds glimmered in her ears. Around her neck, she wore a black lapis stone necklace that accentuated her beauty.

"Coming in as the second runner-up," Victoria continued, "we have Henry Gray."

Once again, applause filled the room as Henry and his family expressed their excitement. Henry had relocated with his family from California to Chicago, his father being an executive at a prominent corporation.

"And last but certainly not least, the winner of the Hemmingbird STEM scholarship is Marcus Davis."

Hearing my name announced, an uncontrollable grin spread across my face. I walked confidently to the podium, feeling a rush of gratitude and joy.

"Before I continue, I must express my deepest thanks to God, my wonderful parents, and especially my dad for always encouraging me to dream big. Thank you, Dad, for everything," I said, looking toward my father, my voice filled with appreciation. Then turning towards my mom, I continued, "And to my incredible mom, thank you for constantly reminding me that I have the power to shape my future. Thank you, Miss Victoria and Mr. Tyrus, for your unwavering support and guidance."

However, filled with sheer excitement, I couldn't resist making a small request. "I have one small favor to ask," I added, eagerness evident in my voice. "Can everyone join me for a photo? It would mean the world to me."

Without hesitation, everyone who had helped organize the dinner enthusiastically gathered around me. I even asked the waiter for assistance.

"Byron, if he could please take a picture."

On my left side were Tyrus and Victoria, and on my right side were my mom and dad. The other two families stood on each side. Once everyone got into position, I exclaimed, "Could everyone say 'college'!" The waiter snapped a photo and then took another one.

"I took two pictures for you, Marcus, just in case one didn't come out," Byron said.

"Thank you, Byron," I expressed my gratitude.

Amidst the excitement, I didn't have the chance to look at the photos. I asked Tyrus and Victoria if I could have a picture with just the two of them. We posed, with Tyrus hugging Victoria and me while resting his hand on my shoulder. Victoria had her arm around my waist, and my dad took the photo. I thanked them both wholeheartedly for everything. Later, I also took pictures with my parents and my friend Henry.

As the evening drew to a close and everyone started leaving the restaurant, Victoria engaged in a conversation with my parents. I approached them after saying goodbye to Henry.

"Congratulations, Mr. Davis!" Victoria beamed at me. "I was just telling your mom and dad that I'd like for you to come down to the lab and see where you'll be doing your internship."

My face lit up like headlights. "Really?" I exclaimed, excited by the prospect. I couldn't contain my enthusiasm, jumping up and down and spinning in a circle. "I can't wait, Ms. Hemmingbird. I can't thank you enough!"

"You've earned it, Marcus," Victoria assured me.

Tyrus walked over and asked, "What's all the excitement about?" My camera started taking random pictures, as if it were stuck, and then abruptly went dead.

"Tyrus, I just invited Marcus to the lab for a tour," Victoria informed him.

"Oh, that's great! You're going to love it down there—it's very cool. I don't know exactly what they do, but it looks fantastic," Tyrus exclaimed, shaking hands with me and my parents. "It was a pleasure to meet both of you, especially you, Marcus. You have a big future ahead of you. Everyone, have a good night." He kissed Victoria on the cheek and waved farewell before leaving.

As I stood there, looking down at my camera and shaking my head, I hoped that my pictures would turn out alright.

"Mr. and Mrs. Davis, I want to thank you for bringing your beautiful family. I've had a wonderful evening with you all," Victoria expressed, extending her hand for a shake. "I'm looking forward to seeing you all soon. Have a wonderful night, and Marcus, we're going to do great things together."

"I hope so—I don't want to disappoint you," I replied, feeling a mix of nerves and excitement. Victoria and I exchanged a laugh as she walked away, engaging in conversation with my mom and dad.

I did notice that my camera acted strangely throughout the night when Tyrus was around, but I chose not to mention it to my parents.

"Mom, dad, what did you think of Miss Hemmingbird?" I looked back at them, curious about their impression.

"She seemed pretty cool," my mom responded.

"Yeah, nice lady, son," my dad said, glancing at me through the rearview mirror. "You know, I think she was kind of interested in me," he added, exchanging a playful look with my mom.

"Paul, nobody wants you but me," my mom retorted.

"And I want you, baby!" My dad blew her a kiss, causing laughter.

"Come on, you guys need to stop," I teased.

"Boy, do you know how you got here?" My dad joked.

"Dad, yeah, I know that, but I don't want to witness any of it. Also, I thought Tyrus was kind of weird," I shared my thoughts.

"He seemed okay, son. He was just on the phone a lot," my mom commented.

"Yeah, Marcus, as your mom said, he was alright," my dad agreed.

Since my camera had died just before Tyrus left, I hadn't been able to review the photos on the ride back home. As soon as I arrived home, I went straight upstairs and plugged in the battery to charge. It took about three hours for the camera to charge fully. While waiting, I relaxed and watched some television. Once the battery was fully charged, I started looking through the photos I had taken at the restaurant.

There were some random images taken when the camera malfunctioned, resembling shadowy shapes of a building. It was quite odd. As I flipped through the photos of my family and friends, I came across the group picture. At that moment, fear washed over me like never before. I couldn't help but exclaim, "Oh my God!"

Hearing my reaction, my mother and father rushed into the room. "Marcus, what's wrong?" My body felt paralyzed as I lay on the bed, horrified by what I saw in the photo.

"It's a group photo, son. What's wrong with it?" My dad asked, picking up the camera.

Realizing that my parents couldn't see what I saw, I quickly came up with an excuse. "Look at me, I'm ugly," I stammered.

"Boy, if you don't stop playing," my mom laughed. "I got you!"

"Boy, you should be in acting school instead of trying to be a scientist," my dad added, playfully hitting me on the back.

My parents left the room, laughing. I picked up the camera again, staring at the group photo. Instead of Tyrus, Fred Hemmingbird stood next to me with one eye closed as if winking at the camera. He had his arm around Tyrus' neck, and Victoria stood beside me. The image was the creepiest thing I had ever seen or felt in my entire life. In another photo, Fred had replaced Tyrus again, but this time, he had his arm around my neck, a knife held up to my throat. I was petrified. I didn't want to leave the house, and I never wanted to see Tyrus again. I kept everything to myself, not sharing what was going on or what I was experiencing. All I could hear was my father's voice saying, "The camera chose you, whatever is happening is meant for you to see." I was utterly terrified, jumping at the slightest noise and constantly looking around nervously.

Two weeks had passed, and my mom had been discussing with me the plan to see Victoria and visit the lab for my internship. The first day of my course was scheduled for Wednesday, May 1, 2019. As a senior, I only had two classes, so I got out of school early. My internship at the STEM lab was set to start at 10:30 AM. The journey from school to the lab in the South Loop area was a long one, involving a train ride and a bus. The Hemmingbird lab itself was a massive, renovated brick warehouse, worth millions of dollars. It had been transformed into a state-of-the-art laboratory, and the building looked magnificent.

Upon arriving at the research center, I entered a wide hallway with dark hardwood floors that gleamed like glass. To my left, there was a large glass map of Chicago with multicolored lights beneath it illuminating the map. The lights changed every 30 minutes, accompanied by the low sound of thunder, rain, lightning, and chirping birds emanating from the overhead speakers. On the right, raised metal letters on a light blue wall spelled out the Hemmingbird research center. That section of the building opened up into a spacious reception area, where I was warmly greeted by the receptionist, Andrea Martinez. She was stunningly beautiful, with long dark hair, red lipstick, and captivating eyes. I couldn't take my eyes off her as she welcomed me.

"Good morning, you must be Marcus," Andrea said with a smile that melted my heart.

"Oh, uh, yes," I stuttered nervously.

"Okay, have a seat. I'll let Victoria know you're here," she said, pointing me towards the chairs on the right side of the room. I continued to gaze at her, momentarily forgetting her instruction.

"I just spoke with Victoria, and she said she'd be right down," Andrea informed me.

"Thank you so much," I replied, finally snapping out of my daze and taking a seat.

The reception area had two large brown double doors, with security officers situated in a small office to the left, where they checked the bags of people entering or exiting the building. It was evident that the facility was highly secure. Moments later, Victoria emerged through the double doors.

"Good morning, Marcus! It's so good to see you," she exclaimed cheerfully, extending her hand for a handshake before pulling me into a warm hug. She then handed me a temporary badge.

"First things first, Marcus. You must wear this badge around your neck or clip it to your clothing at all times when inside the facility. It's the number one rule," Victoria explained.

We went through the double doors, and to the right, we found separate men's and women's restrooms. On the left, there was a locker room where everyone stored their bags, backpacks, and purses, which were checked in by security. From there, we walked along a long hallway with rooms on both sides. After returning from the locker room, stashing away my backpack, I noticed Victoria approaching.

"Good morning, Marcus! Are you ready for the tour?" She asked, full of enthusiasm.

I nodded and followed her lead.

Our journey began as we strolled down a seemingly endless hallway. To our left, we discovered the first room – a delightful break room adorned with vending machines filled to the brim with tempting snacks. Multiple options of cold sandwiches were available, accompanied by a drink machine and a coffee maker brewing a fresh pot of coffee. The room was well-lit, with several tables and chairs beckoning visitors to take a break, while a 40-inch smart television displayed the weather forecast. Peering further down the hallway, we stumbled upon a small storage room, housing a collection of janitorial supplies.

Continuing our expedition, we encountered a set of gray double doors just after entering the building. To the left and right of the doors, two hallways branched off in opposite directions. Directly in front of us, a distinctive room caught our attention. It featured a 4-foot-high wall with glass windows encircling its perimeter, allowing us to peer inside. To our amazement, the room was equipped with five mysterious machines, leaving us curious about their purpose. Two lab-coated gentlemen, with masks covering their noses and mouths, stood inside, with gloves adorning their hands.

Mesmerized, we stood alongside each other, gazing at the gentlemen behind the glass.

Victoria paused outside the window, breaking the silence.

"Okay, Marcus, this is where we conduct our testing on deceased brains, as well as animal brains and similar subjects."

I blinked in astonishment, caught off guard by the revelation.

"Wow, I'm utterly blown away with excitement." She smiled warmly and replied,

"Indeed, it's incredible what we accomplish here. Shall we continue our exploration?"

As we ventured forward, we reached the end of the room, prompting us to encounter a staircase on the right, leading upstairs. The room situated above us was equally intriguing, featuring glass walls that revealed an assortment of animals, including dogs, cats, monkeys, rats, and mice. Blinking in amazement, I couldn't hide my fascination.

Victoria turned to me and asked, "Impressed yet" I grinned widely, unable to contain my excitement. "More than impressed, I'm utterly amazed!"

She nodded understandingly. "I know the feeling. They never cease to impress me either, even after working here for years. But you'll get used to it. We conduct extensive research in this facility."

Exiting the room, we took a right turn and ascended ten stairs before entering Victoria's office. The moment I stepped inside, it reminded me of the time when my father took me on a tour of a submarine during my childhood. To the left of the room, I noticed ten different 20-inch computer monitors, each accompanied by a variety of knobs, gauges, and buttons. Below each screen, there were input and output ports for microphones. Four monitors were turned on, while the other six were powered off. Victoria took a deep breath, the sound of thunder rumbling outside, accompanied by the pattering raindrops on the roof.

"Now, Marcus, let me explain this to you. I know you're going to love this. Each of these monitors provides a live feed of someone's brain. It's an active connection to individuals currently roaming around in Chicago."

I couldn't believe my ears. "What! No way."

"Yes, indeed! It's truly amazing. And now, your internship will involve monitoring brain activities. It's a significant part of your role here, most of which I manage through this computer," she explained, pointing to her own device on the other side of the room. "I'll teach you how to analyze various brain activities, understand emotional states and thoughts of individuals. How does that sound, Marcus?"

I couldn't contain my enthusiasm. "I can't wait to get started!"

"That's what I like to hear; an enthusiastic young man," she replied, beaming with satisfaction.

Three weeks flew by, during which I gradually picked up the skills to interpret brain charts and observed the operations in Victoria's office. I noticed that she often logged into her computer, occasionally leaving me alone in the office for prolonged periods. The sound of her card swiping to unlock the door, followed by her footsteps down the hallway, became familiar to me. There were no surveillance cameras in the office, and an idea started brewing in my mind—I wanted to see the files on her computer. Whether it was my curiosity, nosiness, or an obsession with discovering whose brains I was monitoring on those screens, I couldn't ignore the desire. I found myself ordering a spy pen with a hidden 4K camera and an 8GB storage capacity. With a simple click of a button, it would commence recording. My plan was to discreetly capture Victoria's keystrokes when she signed into her computer, all without arousing any suspicion.

As soon as I arrived home, I rushed upstairs to my room, passing by my parents cooking in the kitchen. Greeting them with a brief exchange, I quickly reached my computer, inserting the tiny SIM card from the pen into my desktop. Reviewing the video, I discovered precisely which keys Victoria pressed. Now armed with the code to access her computer, assuming she hadn't changed it, I contemplated waiting until Friday. On that day, Victoria would only be present in the office once. Friday couldn't come soon enough. With eagerness, I always arrived at the office before her, ensuring that I had an opportunity to explore her computer during her absence.

Friday arrived, and at 1:00 PM, Tyrus Hemmingbird, one of the research facility's visitors, made an appearance. The moment he entered, my nerves got the best of me, causing me to act oddly and avoid eye contact. The memory of our group photos from a previous dinner flashed through my mind, affecting my emotions towards Tyrus with a vague sense of unease. Concerned about my behavior, Tyrus sensed my discomfort.

"Good afternoon, Marcus!" Tyrus greeted me warmly, causing a sharp intake of breath as anxiety coursed through me.

I swallowed hard and replied, "Hi, Mr. Hemmingbird," my voice trembling. "I'm sorry if I seem nervous. It's just that I'm trying my best to do a good job."

Tyrus approached me, placing a comforting hand on my shoulder. My heart skipped a beat, startled by his touch.

"Why so nervous, Marcus? And please, call me Tyrus," he kindly requested.

I stammered in response, unsure of what to say. "I... I don't know."

Tyrus continued observing me, noticing the beads of sweat forming on my forehead. "Are you sure you're alright? You seem to be sweating quite profusely in front of me."

"Yes, sir. I... I apologize. I just feel a little warm sometimes. It's nothing serious," I mumbled, attempting to maintain composure.

Concerned, Tyrus nodded. "Alright, just take it easy, Marcus. Victoria informed me about your excellent work here. I actually came to invite both you and her to lunch, but since she's not around, I'll find someone else to accompany me. Please let her know that I stopped by. Have a good day!"

As Tyrus departed, I felt as though a massive weight had been lifted off my shoulders. The day went by quickly, and after finishing my tasks in Victoria's absence, I found myself captivated by analyzing my own brain activity and status. In that moment, I sensed a peculiar sensation, akin to being a caged animal in the room downstairs, surrounded by fellow creatures undergoing examination. The information I had acquired from Victoria's computer became invaluable as I delved deeper into understanding the implant hidden within my own head. I yearned to discover how it had been placed there without my knowledge, creating a disturbing sense of vulnerability. It was clear that I needed help to remove the chip, and I concluded that conducting further research at home was my next step.

As soon as I arrived home and stepped through the door, I rushed upstairs with haste. In the kitchen, I found my mom and dad busy cooking.

"Good evening, folks," I greeted them.

"Hey, son, how's it going?" My dad responded.

"Everything's good, I just have a few things to check on my computer, that's all." I stood at the foot of the staircase; my backpack slung over my shoulder.

"Take it easy, son, you're rushing too much," my dad cautioned.

In mock exasperation, I started running in slow motion, playfully imitating my dad. "Seriously, Dad, you know you can't beat my $6 million man run."

"Don't hate. You wanted me to slow down," I teased back, glancing at my dad.

Amused by our banter, my parents chuckled as I made my way upstairs to my room, with my dad reminding me to take out the trash.

Upon reaching my room, I sat down at my computer, taking out the small SD card from my pen and inserting it into my desktop. Watching the video, I deciphered the code Victoria had used to secure her desktop. Anticipating Friday, the day Victoria spent the last time in the office, I planned my next move.

On Friday, I arrived at the office early, waiting for Victoria to come in. After she finished her work and left for the day, I discreetly accessed her computer using the code I discovered. Nervously exploring her files, I stumbled upon a document titled "Brainstem Research Applicants," revealing unsettling information. Seeing my name listed as one of the subjects, along with others, sent chills down my spine.

Determined to uncover the truth, I transferred the data to a flash drive but felt overwhelmed by the implications. Desperate for answers, I resolved to investigate further and understand how Victoria had accessed my brain. The thought unnerved me, leaving me feeling like a test subject.

As I reflected on the day's discoveries, I knew I had to delve deeper into the mystery at home. The following Friday, Tyrus unexpectedly appeared at the research facility at 1:00 PM.

"Hi there, Marcus," smiling, "How is it going?"

I instantly felt nervous, sitting in the chair in front of the monitors. Thoughts of the group photos from dinner ran through my mind. My emotions towards Tyrus were very dull and simple; I was scared to death of him. Tyrus had the notion that I was acting strangely because I was avoiding eye contact with him.

"Good afternoon, Mr. Hemmingbird," I said, taking a deep swallow of saliva nervously. It was so quiet that Tyrus heard me swallow. As Tyrus looked at me, sweat began to build upon my forehead.

"Is everything alright, Marcus?" Tyrus asked. "You seem to be sweating profusely. Are you sure you're, okay?"

"Yes, sir, Mr. Hemmingbird. I was just getting a little hot; that's all. It happens from time to time," I replied nervously. Tyrus walked over and touched me across my shoulders as I sat looking at the monitor. I jumped, feeling as if my heart had stopped.

"Why so nervous, Marcus? And stop calling me Mr. Hemmingbird, please. Call me Tyrus."

"I don't know," I replied, hunching my shoulders. "I'm just trying to do a good job, that's all."

"Well, from what Victoria tells me, you're doing a great job," Tyrus said. "I came by to take you and Victoria to lunch, but I should have called first because I see she's not here. So, what do you say, Marcus? Do you want to grab some lunch with me?"

"No, I can't. I have a lot of work to finish up. Besides, I don't want to get in trouble with Victoria."

"Got darn it, okay, no worries. I have a nice date planned with a beautiful lady later. Okay, Marcus, could you please tell Victoria I came by the office? Have a good day."

"OK, I will."

After Tyrus left the office, I felt like the weight of the world had been lifted off my shoulders. Time flew by, and I was on the bus heading home across town. Unbeknownst to me, my nervousness had aroused enough suspicion in Tyrus to start following me around. When I made it back to my computer, I inserted the flash drive and discovered the information Victoria had on me, including a small chip implanted behind my left ear.

There was a tiny incision behind my ear where the chip was placed, unbeknownst to me. I examined the incision with a mirror and learned that Victoria had implanted the device during my interview after I had a drink of apple juice.

She offered me. the device. As I looked at myself in the mirror, I realized I would need help removing the chip. I picked up my cell phone and called my best friend Mark.

"Hey, what's up, Mark?"

"You've got the best hand chief."

"Come over to the house."

"Bet That." Mark arrived at my house just ten minutes after our call. I went downstairs and greeted him at the door.

"What's up Chief."

"You've got the best hand. Come upstairs, I need to show you something." I explained the situation to Mark, and he immediately became concerned.

"What? They turned my partner into a science experiment. Oh no, that's not right." Mark expressed his distress, shaking his head and peering at me through his black-framed glasses, blinking rapidly.

"We can't let them get away with this. I warned you about getting involved with those white people. You know what? I'm going to talk to your parents."

"No, you can't, do that. I'm serious," I urged Mark. as I look at him move his head like a pigeon.

"Why not? They'll find out eventually."

"Only if you spill the beans." I gave Mark a serious look.

"Fine, I'll handle it," I assured him.

"So, what's our plan?" Mark asked while swaying side to side. I instructed him to hold my left ear steady as I made a small incision. As I removed the device with tweezers, Mark's reactions were vivid and dramatic. I stopped momentarily, glancing at his exaggerated expressions.

"Could you try to keep it down?" I requested.

"Alright, got it." Mark complied.

I extracted the device and applied some superglue to the wound. Then, pretending to have a seizure, I startled Mark, who frantically put down the mirror and reached for his phone. Bursting into laughter, I revealed the prank.

"I got you! I got you good," I teased, but Mark's expression remained serious, his blinking uncontrollably.

"Man, stop fooling around. I thought you were in serious trouble," he scolded me.

Holding his baseball hat in his hand, rubbing his forehead and looking at me.

"Boy, you're crazy for real, 911 was going to come and get you. Bet that." I was still laughing hysterically.

"Keep playing, keep playing. Ha, ha, ha! You'll be on the floor, laying right there, dead." I pointed to the floor in the bathroom. "Shaking your ass off. Bet that."

"Man, please, you're just mad because I got you," I said to Mark, giving him the four-combination handshake. "I should have got you with the Alka-Seltzer in my mouth. You would have seen that white foam coming out of my mouth. You would have taken off running."

I took the microchip that I had removed from his head and took a moment to think about what I was going to do with it. We walked downstairs to the kitchen, where I made a couple of bologna sandwiches and put them in a bag, then in my backpack.

We walked over to Mark's house and glued the chip onto the head of his furry dog Bootsy, deep inside his fur so the chip could still be read if Victoria happened to look at it. I knew Tyrus had been following him, though I was unsure of the reason. Tyrus was not good at observing people. I had noticed him following me when I left the lab, following the bus, and even following me after I got off the train.

After gluing the chip to Bootsy, we decided to walk to the park to meet Abe. Before that, we stopped at Walgreens to develop the random shots taken during dinner. I shared with Mark about Tyrus following me and advised him not to panic, though I was unsure of the reason. I had 175 photos developed, as it was a hot, humid day.

Walking through the park, Mark and I found Abe sitting on the steps below the parking lot. I was wearing blue jeans and a Chicago Bulls T-shirt with my backpack. Mark had on blue jeans, a white T-shirt, and a baseball cap.

"What's up, Abe, my man," I greeted him with a high five.

"What's going on, chief," Mark gave him a fist pound.

"Yo, Abe, I brought you a couple of bologna sandwiches," I said, handing them over to Abe.

"Thank you, Marcus, that's good-looking out," Abe replied, glancing back at Mark.

"Man, when did you start talking like your hip?" Mark teased.

"Don't hate, my brother."

I noticed Tyrus standing behind a tree, about 100 yards away, observing everything Mark, Abe, and I were doing through his binoculars. His thoughts seemed dark and ominous, contemplating the idea of violence with a knife. It was clear he had a personal vendetta, particularly towards Abe, as he seemed to recognize his face but couldn't pinpoint from were. Eventually, he made the connection - Abe resembled one of his great-grandfather's old colleagues. A sense of anticipation filled Tyrus as he decided to bide his time and wait for the right moment to exact his revenge.

The heavy police presence made Tyrus cautious, leading him to plan his sinister activities for the next night. Meanwhile, I returned home eager to look through developed photos, hoping to uncover some clues. Mark, unimpressed with the photos, left, leaving me alone in my room. As I examined the images, a sudden realization struck me - they were like pieces of a puzzle waiting to be put together.

Throughout the night, I meticulously arranged the photos, forming a large picture depicting the old factory with Fred standing in front of it. The eerie revelation left me unsettled, gazing out of my window with a sense of dread. Unable to sleep, I heard noises downstairs and found my parents in the kitchen, enjoying a late-night moment with wine and cookies.

Amidst the tension and intrigue, those quiet moments with my family brought a sense of comfort, even in the midst of uncertainty. It was 12:30 in the morning.

"Cool, I'll take some of those good smelling cookies!"

I didn't get to bed until 3:30 that morning. I slept until 1 PM, and my dad left a note with a small bag of clothing by the front door to give to my friend Abe. I called Mark so the two of us could walk down to Griffin Park to drop off the bag of clothing for Abe. However, I tricked Mark into helping with chores around the house, including cutting the grass and other tasks that needed to be done. We didn't make it to the park until 4 PM and found Abe sitting across from the hot dog vendor with a look of longing for a hot dog.

"I walked up to the vendor and ordered four hot dogs with three drinks."

I went to get the hot dogs while Mark chatted with Abe.

"What's up, chief?"

Mark greeted Abe with a fist pump, while sneakily checking out the hot dogs I ordered. After getting the drinks and hot dogs, I nodded to Mark, and we all sat on a park bench, enjoying our food and drinks.

"Abe, here are a couple of pants and long sleeve shirts that my father gave me to give to you. I hope they fit."

"Thanks, Marcus," said Abe, biting into his hot dog. The three of us spent hours talking in the park until it got dark. We told Abe we would catch up with him later in the week and asked him to take care of himself. As we said our goodbyes, Tyrus arrived back at the park. The next night, Tyrus disguised himself in his great-great-grandfather's old trench coat and a blonde wig, while Mark and I bid farewell to Abe and started walking back home.

Tyrus slowly crept towards Abe, who was sitting on a park bench with his back turned, watching the night sky. Suddenly, Abe heard a noise behind him, and as he turned around, he narrowly avoided Tyrus by swinging his knife and cutting his arm. Abe cried out for help, and we rushed back to the scene. Abe was on the ground with someone about to stab him with a knife.

I sprinted towards them, knocking the attacker off Abe. The two of them fell and tumbled, while Mark attempted to run but was hit by a throwing knife in his left hamstring. As Mark fell to the ground, in pain and screaming, Abe tried to flee, only to be chased by Tyrus, who stabbed him in the shoulder, causing him to collapse. In a panic, I threw the bag of clothing at the attacker, dislodging his wig and revealing that it was Tyrus. I called out to Tyrus, asking what he was doing, while

Mark was on the ground with a knife in his leg.

Abe lies face down on his stomach, the knife still in his left leg. Tyrus approaches and, lifting Abe's head, places the blade under his neck.

"Tyrus, please stop. I know what your sister Victoria has done to you. I know about the brainstem," Abe pleads before Tyrus drops his head back onto the grass, standing up and pointing the knife in my direction.

Confused, he questions, "What are you talking about?"

"I discovered that Victoria implanted a chip in both your head and mine. I have a 300-page document detailing everything she has done to you," I explain. Tyrus waves the knife through the air in denial.

"He's not lying. I assisted him in removing the chip from his head just hours ago," Mark interjects, lying on the ground with the knife in his leg.

Tyrus takes deep breaths, composing himself as he observes the blood flowing from Abe's shoulder and speaks in a strong English accent, "So, what do we do now, little black boy? Tyrus is no longer in control."

"What's our next move, Marcus?" Abe inquires, as they all try to make sense of the situation.

Tyrus locks eyes with each of them, then walks over to Mark and forcefully retrieves his knife from his leg, causing Mark to yell out in pain.

"I am the boogie man. If I must return, each of you will meet your end by my hands," Tyrus warns ominously.

"I promised Tyrus that we wouldn't speak a word to

anyone," Mark pleads.

"Tyrus mentioned that my family would be in danger if I failed," Abe adds.

"And you, Marcus," Tyrus addresses, pointing the knife towards me. "I'd be devastated to see anything happen to your beloved Tonya Jenkins. I know more about you than you realize. I saw you leaving her house last night and I am aware of your every move. Your mom and dad are not exempt from harm, Marcus."

With an evil grin and a menacing laugh, Tyrus storms out, leaving in a fit of rage. Upon arriving at the mansion, he notices Victoria's car parked outside. Tyrus bursts through the front door, his eyes fixed on the staircase. Descending to the library, he finds Victoria standing before him. Pulling out his knife from his coat, Tyrus confronts her.

Victoria's gaze locked with Tyrus's intense eyes, filled with questions and concern. "What's going on, Tyrus?" she asked, her voice tinged with worry.

Taking a deep breath, Tyrus maintained a facade of calm mixed with suppressed anger. With a piercing stare, he held Victoria's gaze. "Tell me about the brain stem," he said in a commanding tone, the hint of a broad English accent adding a touch of elegance. "Yes, my beautiful great granddaughter, enlighten us with your knowledge."

As Victoria hesitated, trying to gather her thoughts, the room fell silent, the tension palpable in the air. Suddenly, a loud thump interrupted the moment, causing both of them to startle.

The sound echoed in the room, adding to the suspense that hung heavy between them. Victoria looked puzzled; her curiosity piqued by Tyrus's unexpected request. How would this conversation unfold, she wondered, as she gathered her thoughts to delve into the intricate details of the brain stem.

And so, with the weight of uncertainty looming over them, the exchange between Tyrus and Victoria delved into a realm of knowledge and intrigue, each word spoken opening up a new chapter in their shared history.

As the story unfolded, the complexity of their relationship intertwined with the mysteries of the brain stem, creating a tapestry of emotion and intellect that bound them together in ways they never imagined. And so, in that moment of curiosity and connection, Victoria found herself embarking on a journey of discovery that would forever change her perception of her great grandfather, Tyrus.

Together, they ventured into the depths of knowledge, guided by the unspoken bond that held them together, their shared gaze reflecting a newfound understanding and respect for each other. And as the conversation continued, their voices intertwined in a symphony of intellect and emotion, painting a vivid picture of the intricate workings of the human mind.

In the end, as the last echoes of their discussion faded into the distance, Victoria realized that this encounter was not just about the brain stem—it was about the bonds that connected them, transcending time and space to forge a connection that would withstand the test of time. And with that realization, she knew that her journey with Tyrus and her grandfather was far from over.

The end

About the Author

I was born on South side of Chicago one of 7 Children raised in a Single parent household. I moved to Las Vegas in 1974 and graduated from Eldorado High School in 1982. I begin writing poetry in 1981 and moved back to Chicago 10 years Later.

While studying the works of doctor Malachi Z York for the last 30 years of my life peace and blessings To the Nuwaubian Nation. I never knew my lead pencil would carry me this far. It's so amazing to me how the Universe pulls things out of me whenever I start a poetry piece or a book. Seeing the beginning and the end results of my thoughts knowing that I put my all in my work, satisfies me. I would like to thank everyone that supported me over the years of open mic performances and my books. I hope everyone enjoys this book. Frozen N Time, peace to all. One Love. Donald Townsend.

Contacting the Author

Donald Townsend
email: theflv63@yahoo.com

Books may be ordered from
www.amazon.com
www.gloryboundpublishing.com

Made in the USA
Las Vegas, NV
20 August 2024